Earth's Crust

Grades 6-8

Written by Patricia Urie
Illustrated by S&S Learning Materials

ISBN 1-55035-648-8

Revised January 2006
 "We acknowledge the financial support of the Government of Canada through the Book Publishing Industry Development Program (BPIDP) for this project."

Published in the United States by:
On the Mark Press
3909 Witmer Road PMB 175
Niagara Falls, New York
14305
www.onthemarkpress.com

Published in Canada by:
S&S Learning Materials
15 Dairy Avenue
Napanee, Ontario
K7R 1M4
www.sslearning.com

Learning Expectations	What is Geology?	Inside the Earth	Earth Tectonics	Making Mountains	Earthquakes	Volcanoes	Rocks and Minerals	Fossils	Soil	Research Assignment
Understanding Concepts										
• Describe the composition of the earth's crust	•									
• Recognize patterns as an important concept in geography				•	•	•				
• Identify and describe world landform patterns			•	•	•	•				
• Classify rocks and minerals according to their characteristics and method of formation							•			
• Identify the geological processes involved in rock and mineral formations	•					•	•			
• Explain the rock cycle							•			
• Describe the processes of soil formation									•	
• Describe the processes involved in mountain formation and in the folding and faulting of the earth's surface				•	•	•				
• Analyze evidence of geological change								•		
• Explain the causes of some natural events that happen on or near the surface of the earth		•	•	•	•	•				
• Identify the effects of natural phenomena			•	•	•	•	•		•	
Inquiry/Research & Communication Skills										
• Use appropriate vocabulary, including science and technology terminology, to communicate ideas	•	•	•	•	•	•	•	•	•	•
• Investigate the effect of weathering on rocks and minerals									•	
• Communicate the procedure and results of investigations for specific purposes using written notes, charts/graphs/drawings, and oral presentations					•					•
Map & Globe Skills										
• Identify patterns in physical geography using maps			•	•	•					
• Draw cross-sectional diagrams					•					
Relating Science & Technology to the World Outside the School										
• Identify earth resources used to manufacture products							•			
• Recognize and explain the importance of knowledge of the different types and characteristics of soil in determining its suitability for specific uses									•	
• Identify past and present-day technologies that have contributed to the study of geology				•	•	•				

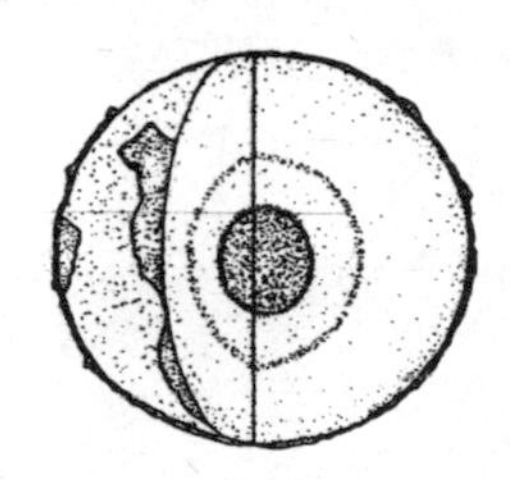

EARTH'S CRUST

Table of Contents

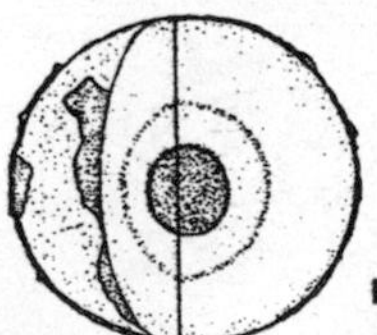

EARTH'S CRUST

Teacher Assessment Rubric

Student Name: Esau

Criteria	Level 1	Level 2	Level 3	Level 4	Level
Understanding Concepts					
• Understands the concepts introduced.	A few	Some	Most	All/almost all	
• Gives complete explanations independently without relying on teacher prompts.	Rarely	Sometimes	Usually	Always/almost always	
Inquiry/Research Skills & Map and Globe Skills					
• Successfully applies required skills.	A few	Some	Most	All/almost all	
• Skills are applied independently without teacher assistance.	Rarely	Sometimes	Usually	Always/almost always	
Communication					
• Uses correct earth science vocabulary introduced.	Rarely	Sometimes	Usually	Always/almost always	
• Communication is clear, accurate, and detailed.	Rarely	Sometimes	Usually	Always/almost always	
Relating Science & Technology to the World Outside the School					
• Understanding of the connections between earth science and the world outside school.	Limited	Some	Good	Thorough	

Comments: ______________________________

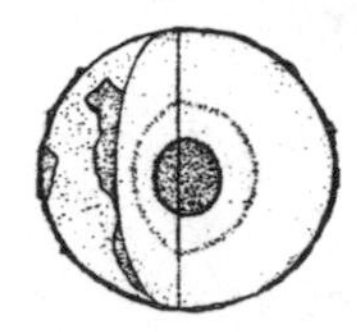

EARTH'S CRUST

Student Self-Assessment Rubric

Name: ESau ______________________ Date: ______________

Put a check mark in each box that most accurately describes your performance, then add your points to determine your total score.

Expectations	Actual Performance (measured in points)				
	1 - Needs Improvement	2 - Sometimes	3 - Frequently	4 - Always/almost always	Points
Understanding Concepts					
I successfully identified, described, and explained the concepts introduced by my teacher.					
I gave complete explanations of concepts, independently without help from my teacher or classmates.					
Inquiry/Research Skills & Map and Globe Skills					
I used maps successfully, and described the procedure and results of investigations.					
I correctly applied these skills independently without needing assistance from my teacher or classmates.					
Communication					
I used the correct earth science vocabulary that was introduced when talking and writing about a subject.					
In my spoken and written communications, I was clear, accurate, and gave lots of detail.					
Relating Science & Technology to the World Outside the School					
I successfully identified, described, and explained the ways in which earth science is connected/related to the world outside school.					

Total Points: ______

Questions for personal reflection:

1. What did you find most interesting, and enjoy learning about the most?
2. What questions do you have now, and what would you like to learn more about?
3. What can you improve upon, and how can you make this improvement?

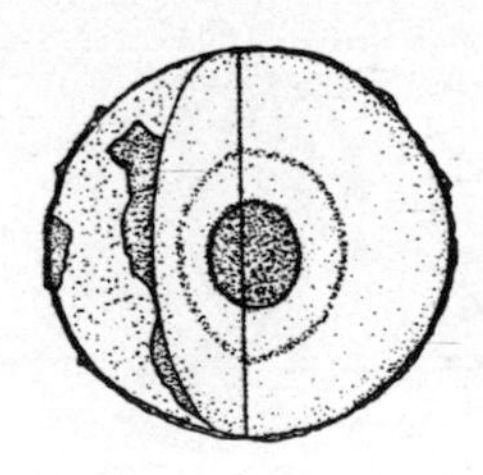

EARTH'S CRUST

Overview

This resouce is divided into nine components. Each component may be used alone or sequentially. At the beginning of each component is a brief overview of the component, a list of resources and answer keys. At the end of this book are four quizzes which cover the material contained in every two components. Quiz number four includes the last three components. This book was designed to provide background information to accompany a study of the earth's crust. Ideally, it should be supplemented with simple experiments and a good deal a research by the students. Research topics can be found at the end of the book.

Component	This component examines the concepts related to...
What is Geology?	• an introduction to the science of geology and the job of the geologist
Inside the Earth	• the composition of the layers of earth, composition, lithosphere, asthenosphere
Earth Tectonics	• the theories of plate tectonics and continental drift, identifying the major tectonic plates, the Mid-Atlantic Ridge
Making Mountains	• the processes involved in the formation of fold, dome, block-fault and volcanic mountains
Earthquakes	• earthquakes: where they occur and why, the Ring of Fire, measurement of, seismology, effects of quakes
Volcanoes	• the process involved in the formation of volcanoes, different types of volcanoes, hot spots, geysers, the Ring of Fire
Rocks and Minerals	• the three major types of rocks, identifying minerals, the rock cycle
Fossils	• the formation of fossils, their importance to the earth sciences, the major geological eras of the earth
Soil	• how soil is formed, the composition and characteristics of soil

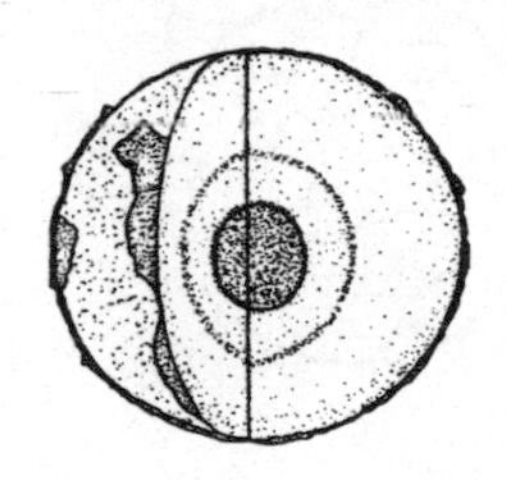

EARTH'S CRUST

Implementation Suggestions

1. Before beginning the book, read through it to determine what additional activities, such as simple experiments etc., could supplement the reading cards. Having a good knowledge of the contents will help when ordering films and collecting books and other items for display.

2. Consider planning a trip to a museum or science center to see exhibits of rocks, minerals, fossils, etc.

3. The reading cards can be mounted for group work and stored for future groups. The work sheets (Info Check) can be copied or put on the overhead. If put on the overhead, their format will help the students as they try to lay out and organize their work.

4. Plan to have the students involved in as much research as possible. They will need access to numerous books, electronic encyclopedias, etc.

5. Locate or order any suitable films or filmstrips.

6. Collect pictures or charts, postcards of rocks, interesting geological features such as mountains, rivers, streams, volcanoes, earthquakes, canyons, geysers, etc.

7. The blank cards can be used to make activity cards.

8. The research topics pages can be cut up and pasted onto individual cards and laminated, or given to the students as is.

9. Ask students, parents and colleagues for any items such as rocks, minerals, pictures, fossils, etc. that might add to a display.

10. Collect items such as rocks, minerals, fossils, lava, sand, globes, soil test kits, soil, balance scales for weighing rocks, soil samples, microscopes, and crystals.

11. Begin to collect news items about volcanoes, earthquakes, etc.

12. Collect as many books as possible; only a few have been listed in the resources. Some key words and topics are: geology, earth science, volcanoes, earthquakes, mountains, soil, fossils, gemstone, rivers, erosion rocks, and minerals. Note: a short list of resources suitable for each component has been placed on the teacher input sheet for quick reference. Many earth science books contain simple experiments that can be carried out in the classroom with simple materials.

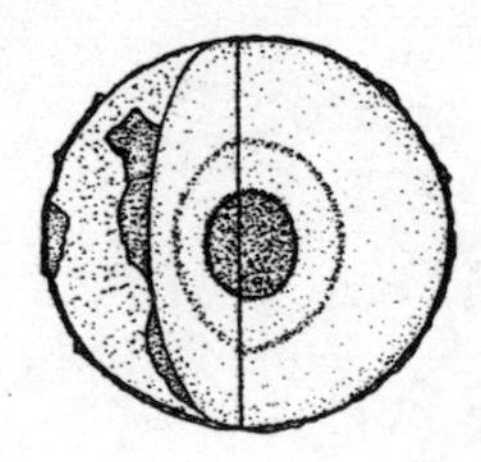

EARTH'S CRUST

13. Consider art activities related to this research such as:

    a) Rock painting (smooth beach rocks are good sources)
    b) Drawing a rock
    c) Sand pictures (sand can be bought or colored, or powdered tempera paint can be added)
    d) Rock sculptures (try using a hot glue gun!)

14. Integrate language activities by researching myths and legends about volcanoes and earthquakes, etc. Students could retell orally or in writing some of these myths, or write their own. The reading cards and Info Check pages make good reading comprehension material.

15. Set up a center in the classroom where students can use balance scales and spring scales, etc. to weigh and compare different types of rocks. Great rock samples, lava, etc., can usually be found in pet or aquarium stores.

16. Rock collections can be placed in egg cartons for classification and identification activities.

17. Rent a traveling rock, mineral, or fossil collection from a museum for use in the classroom.

18. Punch these pages and place in a binder for easy access and storage of other related items.

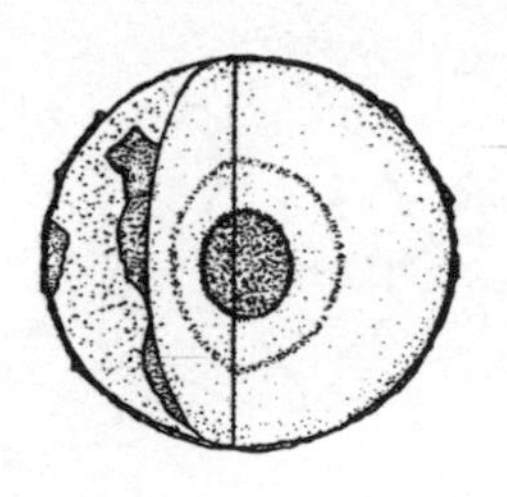

EARTH'S CRUST

Vocabulary

bedrock
biological
chemical
clay
cleavage
composition
continental drift
crust
earthquakes
erosion
fault
fossil
geology
humus
igneous rock
interior
lava
luster
magma
mantle
mechanical weathering
metamorphic rock
mineral
mining
molten
mountain
oceanic
paleontologist
particles
pedologist
plate
porosity
ridge
rock cycle
sediment
sedimentary
seismic wave
seismology
seismometer
shield volcano
silt
soil
strata volcano
subduction
texture
tectonic
theory
topography
tremor
volcano
weathering

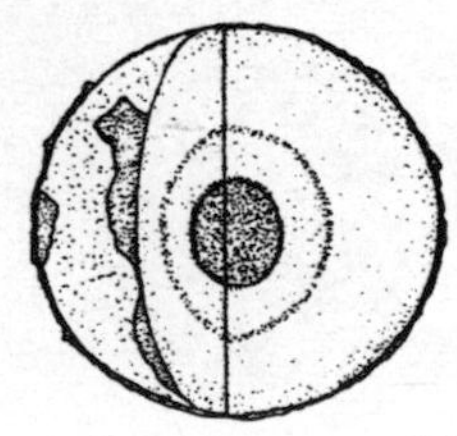

EARTH'S CRUST

Name: ______________________________

My Vocabulary

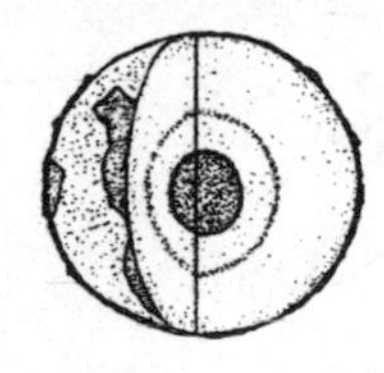

EARTH'S CRUST

Student Observation

Date: ____________ ______________________________

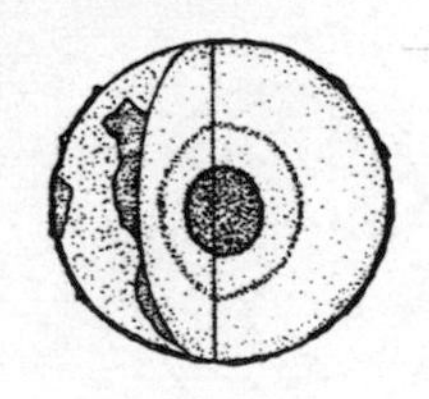

EARTH'S CRUST

Name: ______________________________

Student Self-Tracking Sheet

Topic	All Activities Completed ✓	How I Did 1 - Had difficulty 2 - Fair 3 - Good 4 - Very good	Quiz Score
What is Geology?			
Inside the Earth			
Earth Tectonics			
Making Mountains			
Earthquakes			
Volcanoes			
Rock and Minerals			
Soil			
Research			

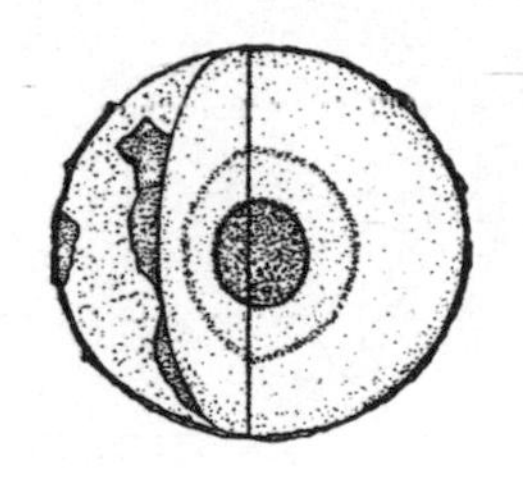

EARTH'S CRUST

What is Geology?

Teacher Input

Overview

This component acts as an introduction to the study of the earth's crust by familiarizing the students with the science of geology and the job of the geologist. A related film about the earth or a brainstorming session to assess what knowledge the students have of the earth would be appropriate before assigning the information cards and follow-up activities. As this component requires the students to use a dictionary to investigate word meanings, some of the written work could be included as part of a Language Arts block.

Resources

Berger, Melvin. The New Earth Book. Thomas Y. Crowell; New York, ©1980.

Braus, Judy. Geology: The Active Earth. National Wildlife Federation; Washington D.C., ©1988.

Burns, George. Exploring the World of Geology. Grolier Pub.; New York, ©1995.

Farndon, John. How the Earth Works. Reader's Digest Assoc; New York, ©1992.

Hehner, Barbara. Blue Planet: The Forces that Shape Our World. Somerville House Pub.; Toronto, ©1992.

Markle, Sandra. Digging Deeper. Lothrop, Lee and Shepard Books; New York, ©1987.

McConnell, Anita. The World Beneath Us. Facts on File Inc.; New York, ©1985.

Parker, Steve. The Earth and How It Works. MacMillan of Canada; Toronto, ©1989.

Thackray, John. The Earth and Its Wonders. Larousse and Co.; New York, ©1980.

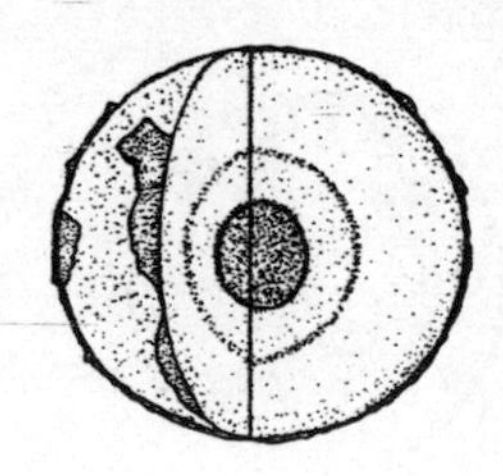

EARTH'S CRUST

What is Geology?

Answers

Info Check: *(page 17)*

1. a) ***theory*** – an idea or set of ideas made up to explain why something happened or continues to happen
   b) ***origin*** – the beginning of something
   c) ***predict*** – to tell what will happen before it happens
   d) ***formation*** – the act or process of the development of something

2. a) geology b) biology c) crystallography d) seismology
   e) meteorology f) astronomy g) volcanology h) paleontology
   i) anthropology j) mineralogy

3. a) bio – life b) geo – earth c) eco – home d) thermo – heat
   e) astro – stars

4. rocks, minerals, earthquakes, fossils, soils, crystals, volcanoes, geothermal energy, mountains, faults, the interior of the earth, coal, oil, seismic waves, geysers, etc.

5. Answers may vary – should make reference to helping locate and monitor use of earth's resources, understand and hopefully predict earthquakes and volcanoes to save lives, etc.

Geowords: *(page 19)*

1. e 2. c 3. a 4. q 5. j 6. b 7. h 8. k
9. g 10. m 11. l 12. p 13. n 14. i 15. o 16. d
17. f

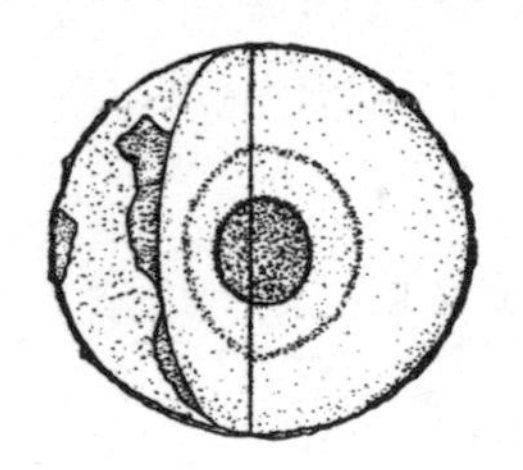

EARTH'S CRUST

What is Geology?

Information Card #1

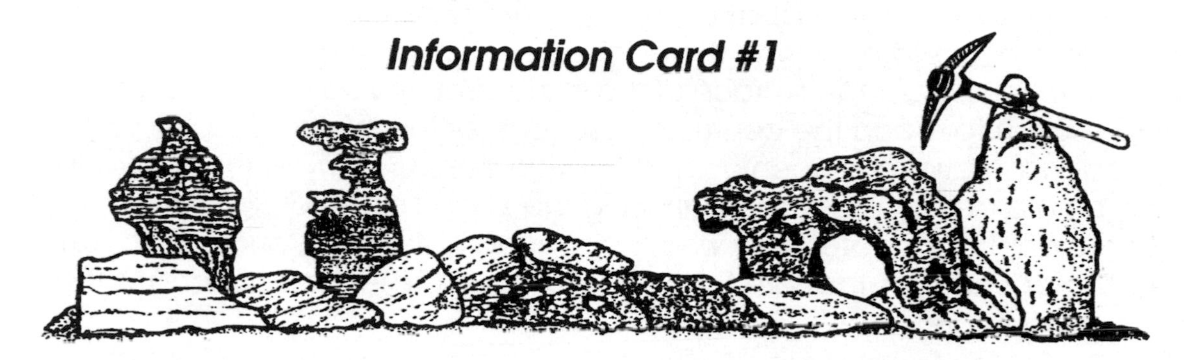

Throughout the ages, people have tried to understand the planet on which we live. Ancient peoples explained the things they saw happening on the earth through myths and legends. The ancient Hindus believed the earth was carried on the back of an elephant. The elephant stood on a turtle and the turtle stood on a cobra. The earth would tremble and shake whenever one moved! The ancient Japanese believed earthquakes were caused by Namazu, a giant catfish which lived beneath the ground. When Namazu shook its body, the earth would tremble and break open. Some, like the ancient Greeks, believed that angry gods made volcanoes erupt. The Romans thought their god of fire, Vulcan, lived beneath Mt. Etna where he made thunderbolts for the god Jupiter!

People always ask questions and seek answers to things that can't be explained. One group of people always searching for answers about the earth are scientists. Scientists continually investigate the earth looking for answers, and although the scientific knowledge of the earth has increased greatly, there is still much to learn about the inside of our planet.

The study of the earth beneath us is known as the science of geology. The word 'geology' comes from the ancient Greek work 'geo', which means earth. Geologists are scientists who study the origins and development of the earth, as well as its size, shape, and composition. They study the processes which have changed the earth's surface over millions of years, and the forces that continue to change the earth's surface today. Little is known about the inside of the earth as scientists have not been able to fully penetrate even the crust, the thinnest layer of the earth.

Over the years, many scientists have developed theories about the earth. A Scottish geologist named James Hutton (1726 – 1797) is called the founder of modern geology. Hutton challenged the belief of his day that the earth was only 6 000 years old. Hutton insisted it was much older, and theorized that the earth's crust was constantly changing. Scientists have learned that Hutton was correct. The earth's crust is constantly changing!

EARTH'S CRUST

The earth's crust is the hard outer layer which covers the surface of the earth. It ranges from 8 to 64 km (5 to 40 mi) in thickness, and even though it is covered with oceans, lakes, valleys, plains and mountains, it is a very thin layer. As scientists study the geological processes and events such as volcanoes, earthquakes and mountain building, they have determined that everything that happens on the earth's crust is directly related to forces from inside the earth. Geologists have only been able to dig about 16 km (10 mi) below the surface of the earth. You would have to dig nearly 6 500 km (4 000 mi) to reach the center, and so most of the information geologists have about the earth's interior has been gained through careful study of the geologic events happening on the earth's crust. By examining the earth's crust for signs of ancient eruptions, geologists can determine what happened in the past, and gain a better understanding of changes that are taking place in the present and changes that may take place in the future!

Geologists depend on many other branches of science to assist them in their investigations. Biologists, physicists, astronomers, mineralogists, microscopists, pedologists, crystallographers and paleontologists, to name a few, all contribute specialized information about the earth. As scientists accumulate knowledge and put it all together, they are gaining a better understanding of our planet.

As they study the rocks that make up the entire surface of the planet, geologists are able to predict where coal, oil, water, iron, ore, and certain valuable minerals might be found. We depend on minerals from the earth for fuel, building materials, and raw materials for many industries. Geologists are able to assist in the location and identification of useful rocks and minerals as well as precious stones like rubies, diamonds and emeralds. They are often hired by oil and mining companies as well as by the government to carry out geological surveys. Geologists are able to determine whether or not we are making the best use of the earth's resources, and how our activities may be depleting these resources. Their expert knowledge of rocks and soils are very useful when decisions are made about where to build bridges, towers, tunnels and dams, etc.

As paleontologists, scientists who study fossils, investigate the composition of the layers of the earth, they are able to determine the types of plant and animal life that lived in an area, sometimes millions of years ago. By studying fossils, the remains of plants and animals embedded in rock, they can determine what the earth must have been like at different times in the geologic history of the earth.

Much of the knowledge and theories that scientists have developed about the earth have come from studying geological events such as earthquakes and volcanoes. By studying volcanoes and earthquakes, and the processes involved in their formation and eruption, volcanologists and seismologists are sometimes able to predict future catastrophes and perhaps save lives and property.

By putting all their records together and comparing them, scientists are able to learn more about the processes that are constantly changing the face of our planet.

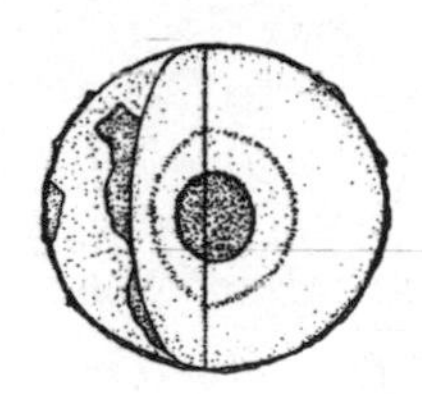

EARTH'S CRUST

What is Geology?

Info Check

1. Write definitions for the following words:

   a) theory: A bunch of ideas used to explain somthing.

   b) origin: The Start of something i.e a Building.

   c) predict: To guess Something i.e the weather.

   d) formation: The process of developing something

2. Match each science with the special area studied.

   a) Geology the study of the earth's crust
   b) BIology the study of living things
   c) Crystallography the study of crystals
   d) seismology the study of earthquakes
   e) meteorology the study of the weather
   f) Astronomy the study of stars and planets
   g) volcanology the study of volcanoes
   h) paleontology the study of fossils
   i) Anthropology the study of humankind
   j) Mineralogy the study of minerals

crystallography
seismology
mineralogy
geology
biology
paleontology
anthropology
volcanology
meteorology
astronomy

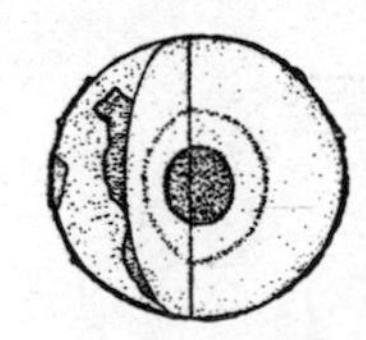

EARTH'S CRUST

3. Many scientific words come from the ancient Greek and Latin languages. Try to match the Greek or Latin words with their meaning. Write three words containing each prefix.

life **earth** **home** **heat** **stars**

a) *life* bio - *biology* ______, ______

b) Earth geo - geology, ______, ______

c) Home eco - ecology, ______, ______

d) Heat thermo - thermology, ______, ______

e) stars astro - astronomy, ______, ______

4. List aspects of the earth that are of special interest to a geologists.

a) Rocks

b) minerals

c) Earthquakes

d) Fossils

e) soils

f) crystals

g) geothermal

h) Volcanoes

i) energy

j) oil

5. Explain the importance of the science of geology.

The importance of the science of geology is to hopefully predict earthquakes and volcanoes to help save peoples lives.

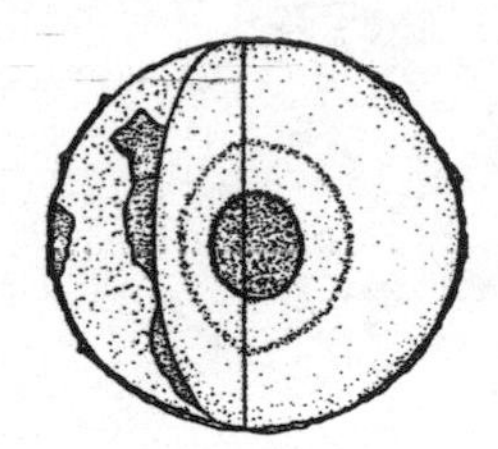

EARTH'S CRUST

What is Geology?

Geowords

Geology comes from the Greek word 'geo' which means 'earth'. Listed below are several 'geo' words. Match each word to its meaning. Before you check with your dictionary, try to figure out the definitions on your own!

	My Guess	Definition	related to ____________ of the earth
a) geocentric	1. E	1. E	the features, life and human activity
b) geochemistry	2. C	2. C	the order of geologic events
c) geochronology	3. A	3. A	or measured from the center
d) geocorona	4. g	4. g	or resembling the shape or surface
e) geography	5. j	5. j	the internal heat
f) geology	6. B	6. B	the composition and alteration of the solid matter
g) geophone	7. H	7. H	any science
h) geoscience	8. K	8. K	the growth of an organism in response to gravity
i) geotectonic	9. g	9. g	seismic vibrations (device used to measure)
j) geothermal	10. M	10. M	agriculture
k) geotropism	11. L	11. L	high pressure inside
l) geopressured	12. p	12. p	the magnetism
m) geoponic	13. N	13. N	physics and environment
n) geophysics	14. I	14. I	shape, structure of rock masses of the crust
o) geomorphology	15. O	15. o	the size and shape
p) geomagnetism	16. D	16. D	the outermost region of the atmosphere
q) geodesic	17. F	17. F	evolution and form of landforms

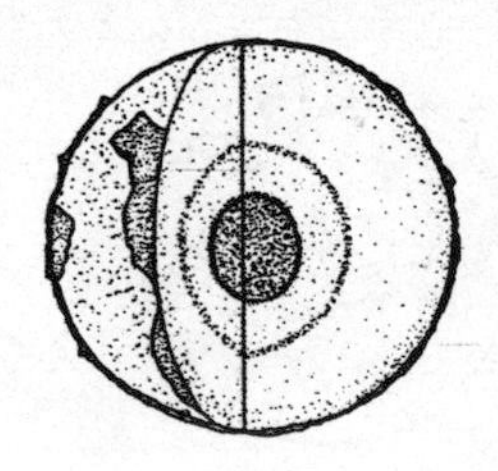

EARTH'S CRUST

Inside the Earth

Teacher Input

Overview

This component familiarizes the students with the composition of the earth. They investigate the layers of the earth and become familiar with the scientific terms, data and theories associated with the composition of the earth. The students are introduced to seismology and the role it plays in helping to provide information about the earth's interior. The terms 'lithosphere' and 'asthenosphere' are introduced as they are important to the students' understanding of the concepts related to tectonic plates and continental drift presented later.

Resources

Berger, Melvin. The New Earth Book. Thomas Y. Crowell; New York, ©1980.

Thackray, John. The Earth and Its Wonders. Larousse and Co.; New York, ©1980.

McConnell, Anita. The World Beneath Us. Facts on File Inc.; New York, ©1985.

Parker, Steve. The Earth and How It Works. MacMillan of Canada; Toronto, ©1989.

Parker, Steve. The Marshall Cavendish Science Project Book of the Earth. Marshall Cavendish Pub.; New York, ©1986.

Farndon, John. How the Earth Works. Reader's Digest Assoc.; New York, ©1992.

Markle, Sandra. Digging Deeper. Lothrop, Lee and Shepard Books; New York, ©1987.

Hehner, Barbara. Blue Planet: The Forces that Shape Our World. Somerville House Pub.; Toronto, ©1992.

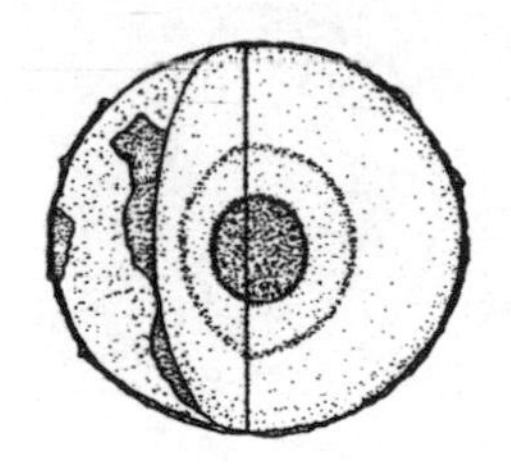

EARTH'S CRUST

Inside the Earth

Answers

Info Check: *(page 24)*

1. a) ***earthquake*** – a shaking of the ground caused by sudden movement of rock far beneath the surface of the earth
   b) ***resource*** – something that is a source of wealth for a country
   c) ***lithospere*** – the crust and rigid upper layer of the mantle which float on the asthenosphere
   d) ***asthenosphere*** – the lower, very molten part of the mantle upon which the lithosphere floats
   e) ***seismic wave*** – the vibration that is released during an earthquake

2. Scientists are not able to penetrate very far into the earth's crust.

3. **thinnest** – crust **thickest** – mantle **densest** – inner core

4.

No.	Earth Layer	Description
b)	crust	thinnest, 5-40 km (3 – 25 mi) thick, supports life on earth
c)	upper mantle	together with crust forms lithosphere
a)	lithosphere	crust and upper mantle together, float on asthenosphere
d)	asthenosphere	molten, moves by convection currents
f)	inner core	consists of iron and nickel, solid due to pressure of other layers
e)	outer core	molten, mostly iron with some nickel, flows

5. a) ***sulphur*** – a chemical element, yellow, often comes up with magma and is deposited in the craters of volcanoes, bad smell when burned, used to make matches and gunpowder, fertilizers, plastics
   b) ***iron*** – a chemical element, hard, strong brittle metal, commonly found in the minerals hematite and pyrite, used to make steel and stainless steel
   c) ***nickel*** – a chemical element, hard silvery metal, corrosion resistant, used to make money and mixed with other metals, mined in northern Ontario
   d) ***granite*** – igneous rock, continents are mostly granite, Canadian shield made of granite, one of the most useful rocks in the world because of its strength, used to make foundations, piers, sea walls, can be cut into almost any shape and polishes well, used for monuments and buildings

EARTH'S CRUST

Inside the Earth

Information Card #2

People have always wondered what the inside of the earth is like. The ancient Greeks believed it was Hades, the world of the dead. In his famous book, Journey to the Center of the Earth, science fiction writer, Jules Verne, depicted the inside of the earth as a place of great crystal caverns and prehistoric monsters. With all the knowledge scientists have gained about the earth over the years, little is really known about the interior of the earth. Scientists can only study the crust of the earth for clues and theories about what is at the heart of our planet.

Most of the information geologists have about the inside of the earth has been gained from studying the geologic events that occur on the earth's crust, especially earthquakes. Investigating earthquake waves is one of the few ways geologists have of learning about the inside of the earth.

Earthquakes are caused by sudden shifts of rock on or near the surface of the earth. These shifts produce waves of energy called 'seismic waves', which spread out in many directions. Seismic waves from an earthquake travel through the earth like sound waves travel through the air, and are recorded with special instruments called seismographs. Seismologists record these waves at different places on the earth's surface, and collect information about ground movements before, during, and after an earthquake. As waves pass through different substances in different ways, scientists are able to make very good guesses about the composition of the earth.

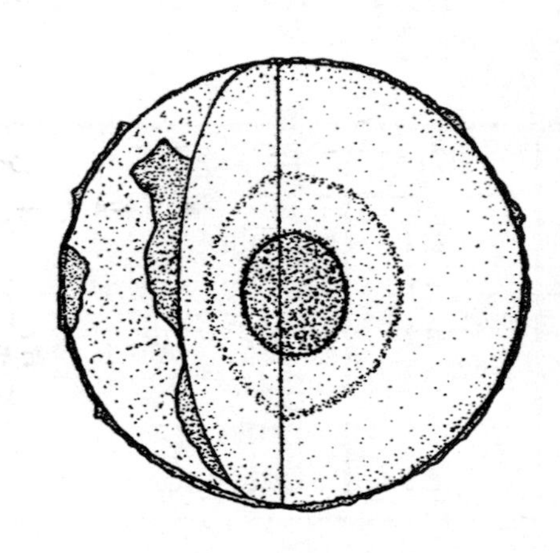

Scientists know that various types of earthquake waves travel at different speeds through different rocks. They change direction as the pass from one layer to another. The waves travel faster in high-density mantle then they do in the crust, which consists of lighter material. When the waves pass from one material to the other, they bend and are bounced back, depending on the substance they are going through. Seismologists record these waves at different places on the earth's surface. By recording where the shock waves arrived, the angle at which they emerged, and the time it took for them to arrive, scientists have an idea of the type of material they passed through. By putting all their records together and comparing them, scientists are able to learn more about what is happening inside the earth. By comparing many seismological records, scientists have been able to theorize about the composition of the earth's interior. They have an idea of how far below the earth's surface each layer is, its thickness, and its composition.

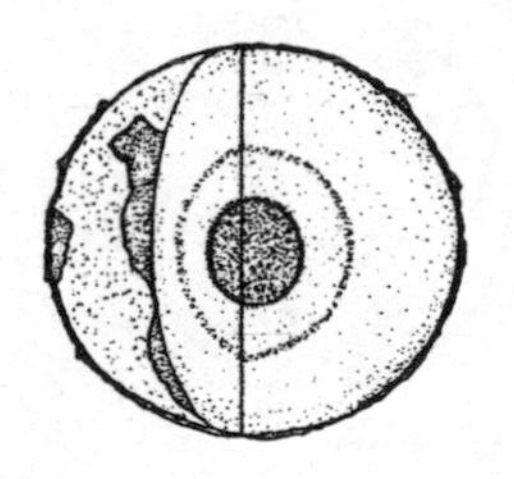

EARTH'S CRUST

Cutting into the earth, we would pass through three layers. All the landforms of the earth, such as mountains, hills, valleys, and plains, are part of the first layer, the earth's 'crust'. It is the crust which supports all life and from which we obtain many of the resources we use for survival on our planet. The earth's crust makes up less than 1 percent of the earth's volume, and varies in thickness from about 5 km (3 mi) under the oceans, to about 40 km (25 mi) at its greatest depth. If we compared the earth to an apple, the crust of the earth, which makes up our continents and the ocean floors, is thinner than the skin on the apple.

The layer beneath the crust is called the 'mantle' and accounts for approximately 83 percent of the earth's volume. The mantle is a thick layer which is about 2 900 km (1 800 mi) deep. The upper part of the mantle is solid like the crust and, along with the crust, makes up the geological region called the 'lithosphere'. The lower part of the mantle has much higher temperatures and pressure. The rock in the lower part of the mantle is melted or 'molten', and it is thought that it flows slowly. This molten part of the mantle is called the 'asthenosphere'.

The core is even hotter than the mantle and makes up about 16 percent of the earth's volume, and 32 percent of the earth's weight. The core consists of two regions: the 'outer core' and the 'inner core'. The inner core, or center of the earth, is made of iron and nickel, and because of the extremely high pressure geologists believe it is probably solid. The inner core is thought to be 2 500 km (1 500 mi) across while the outer core is about 2 200 km (1 300 mi) thick. Because of the high heat, the outer core is thought to be very liquid. Geologists believe the outer core flows very slowly and forms the magnetic field of the earth.

Research Challenge!

Do some research and find out the temperatures of the different layers of the earth's interior. You may discover that the information in different reference books varies. What reasons can you think of to explain this?

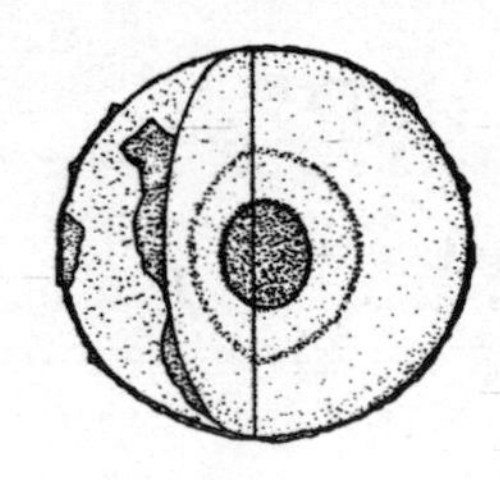

EARTH'S CRUST

Inside the Earth

Info Check

1. Write definitions for the following words:

   a) earthquake: A Terrible shake in the ground.

   b) resource: A big source of wealth that is traded throughout countrys.

   c) lithosphere: The crust and rigid upper layer of the mantle which floats on the asthenosphere.

   d) asthenosphere: The lower, extremely molten part of the mantle upon the lithosphere floats on

   e) seismic wave: A wave that's unleashed during a Earthquake.

2. Why is little known about the interior of the earth? Scientists can't penetrate into the Earth's crust.

3. Which layer of the earth is the thinnest? Crust
   thickest? Mantle
   densest? Inner core

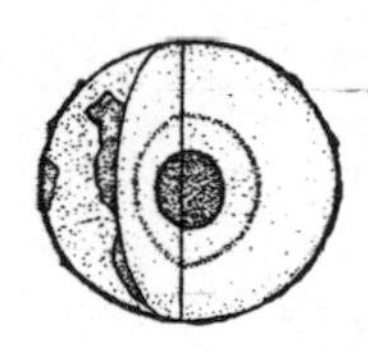

EARTH'S CRUST

4. Complete the diagram below to illustrate the inside of the earth. Color the diagram so that each layer is clearly shown.

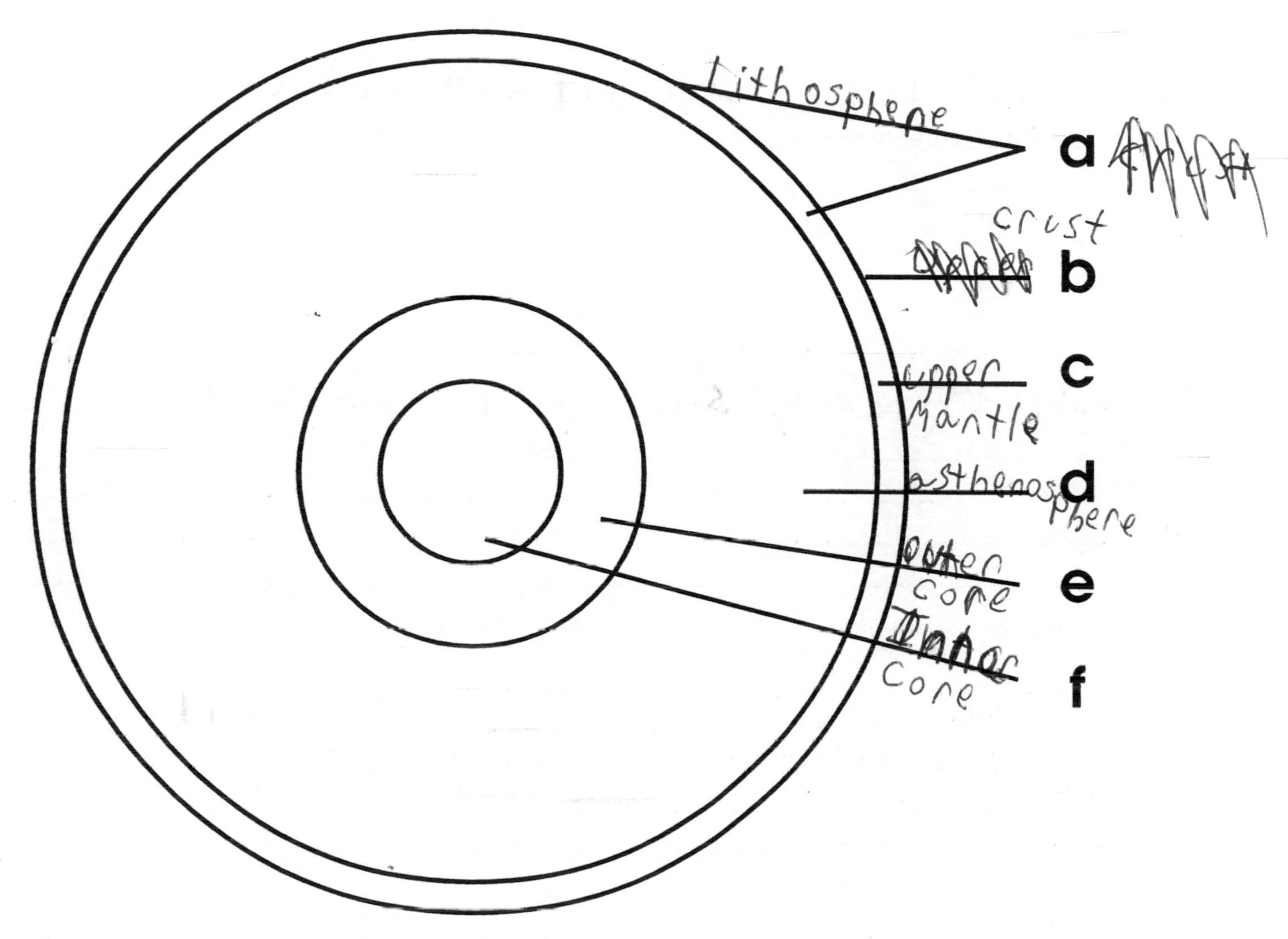

Letter	Earth Layer	Description
B	crust	Thinnist 5-40 km (3-25 mi) thick, supports all life on Earth.
C	upper mantle	Together with crust makes lithosphere
A	lithosphere	Crust and upper mantle together floats on asthenosphere
D	asthenosphere	Molten, moves by convection currents
F	inner core	Consists of iron and nickle, solid due to the other layer
E	outer core	Molten mostly iron and some nickel, flows

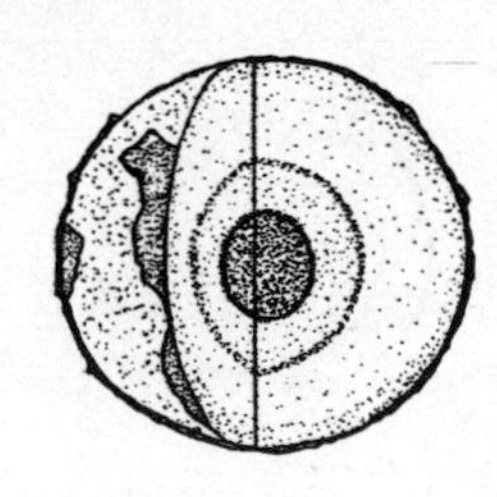

EARTH'S CRUST

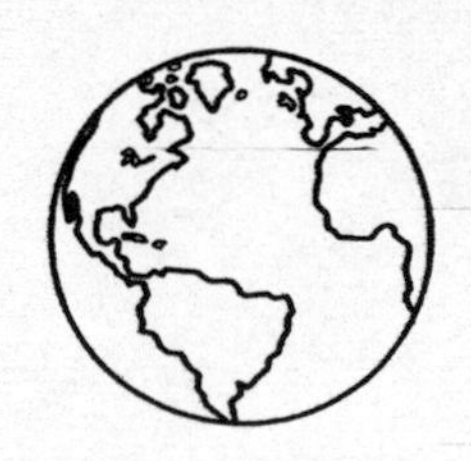

5. Different layers of the earth consist of different types of rocks and minerals. Do some research to find information about each of the following:

a) sulphur: a chemical element yellow oftEn comes up with magma.

b) iron: a extremely strong peice of metal.

c) nickel: a chemical element, a hard silvery metal corrosion resistant and is used to make money.

d) granite: A really strong rock used to make piers, sea walls, monuments and buildings.

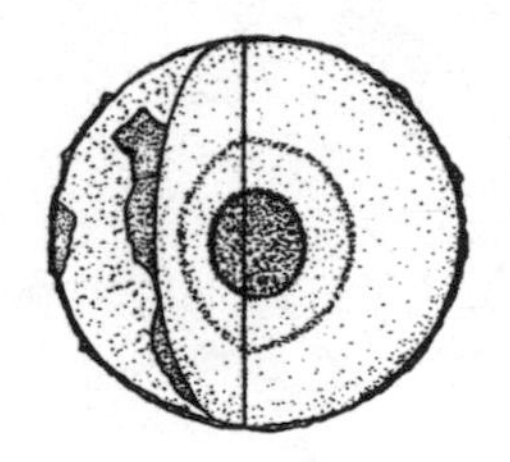

EARTH'S CRUST

Earth Tectonics

Teacher Input

Overview

This component introduces a key concept in a study of the earth's crust, namely, the theory of plate tectonics. The students investigate plate tectonics and the information scientists have gained to support the theory. They are familiarized with Pangaea, the supercontinent, and the theory of continental drift. Using maps and atlases, they become familiar with the location of the major tectonic plates, and the impact their movement has on the shaping of the earth's surface.

Resources

Berger, Melvin. The New Earth Book. Thomas Y. Crowell; New York, ©1980.

McConnell, Anita. The World Beneath Us. Facts on File Inc.; New York, ©1985.

Parker, Steve. The Earth and How It Works. MacMillan of Canada; Toronto, ©1989.

Braus, Judy. Geology: The Active Earth. National Wildlife Federation; Washington, D.C., ©1988.

Farndon, John. How the Earth Works. Reader's Digest Assoc.; New York, ©1992.*
*(an excellent resource for hands-on experiences and experiments)

Markle, Sandra. Digging Deeper. Lothrop, Lee and Shepard Books; New York, ©1987.

Rogers, Daniel. Earthquakes. Raintree Steck-Vaughn; Texas, ©1999.

Nicolson, Cynthia Pratt. Earthdance. Kids Can Press; Toronto, ©1994.

Nixon, Hershell. Earthquakes: Nature in Motion. Dodd Mead; New York, ©1981.

Vrbova, Zuza. Volcanoes and Earthquakes. Eagle Books Ltd.; New Jersey, ©1990.

Hehner, Barbara. Blue Planet: The Forces that Shape Our World. Somerville House Pub.; Toronto, ©1992.

Walker, Sally M. Earthquakes. Carolrhoda Books; Minn., ©1996.

Dudman, John. Earthquake. Wayland Pub.; England, ©1992.

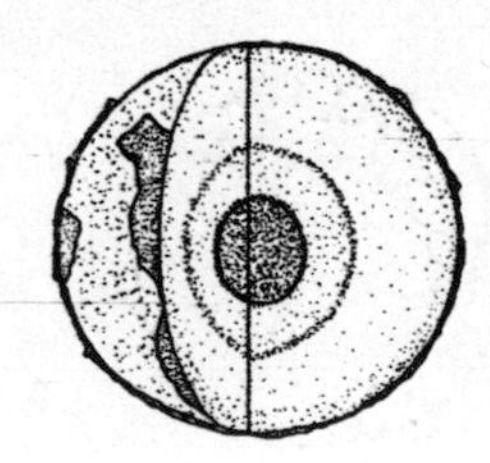

EARTH'S CRUST

Earth Tectonics

Answers

<u>Info Check</u>: *(page 31)*

1. Wegener – see Information Card #3 (p. 29, 2nd paragraph)
2. In later years, fossil evidence and the Mid-Atlantic Ridge were discovered. This evidence supported Wegener's theory of a large super continent which had separated over millions of years.
3. Pangaea – means 'all lands'
4. Continental Drift – the continents are located on top of huge tectonic or lithospheric plates, which are constantly moving because they float on the soft, molten layer of the mantle called the asthenosphere.
5. a) Pacific plate
   b) North American and Eurasian plates
   c) Eurasian and the Indo-Australian plates
   d) African and Arabian plates
6. The Atlantic Ocean is constantly getting wider because the North American plate and the Eurasian plate are moving away from each other. Magma is constantly oozing out of the crack between these two plates and forming new ridges on the ocean floor. As new ridges are formed, the ocean floor spreads.
7.

Name of Plate	Direction of Movement
North American	north west
Eurasian	south west
South American	west
Indo-Australian	north west
Pacific	west
African	north east

8. & 9.

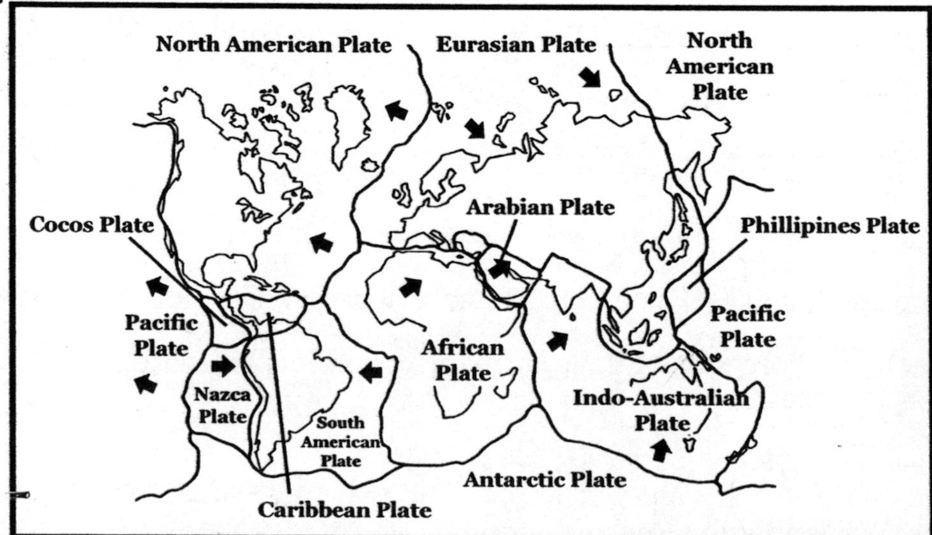

10. Answers will vary, however it is believed that the continents will meet again to form one large land mass and that this has happened several times since the earth was formed. It is believed that it takes approximately 440 million years for each cycle.

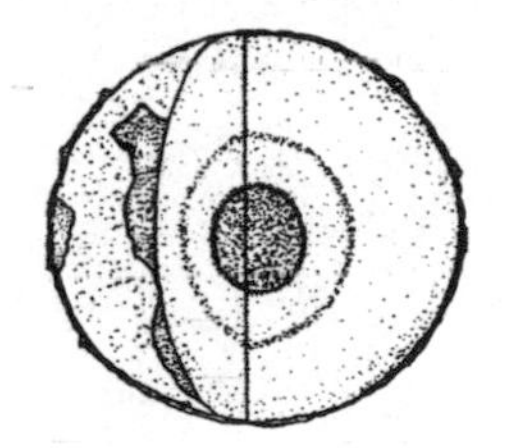

EARTH'S CRUST

Earth Tectonics

Information Card #3

Geologists know the earth's crust is changing all the time. It is moved from side to side and tilted upwards and downwards by forces from inside the earth. Sudden movements cause powerful earthquakes to shake the earth and volcanoes to erupt. Islands and mountains are formed when pressure causes the earth's crust the wrinkle.

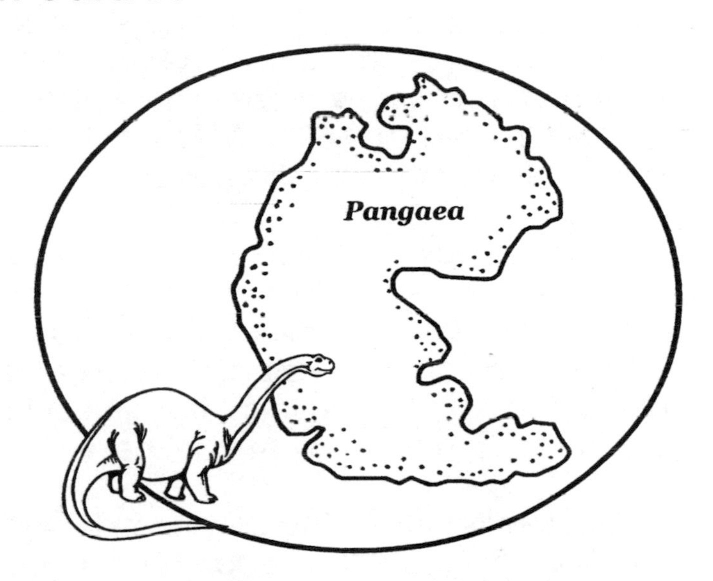

Geology theorizes that millions of years ago the continents were once all joined together as one supercontinent. This theory was first presented in 1923 by a meteorologist, named Alfred Wegener. Wegener proposed the theory that the continents are constantly moving, drifting over the surface of the earth. He believed they were once a part of a single supercontinent which he named "Pangaea", meaning "all lands". Wegener theorized that about 200 million years ago, when the dinosaurs were appearing on the earth, Pangaea started to split apart. Slowly, over millions of years, masses of land broke away from Pangaea forming the continents. The portion holding North America and Eurasia moved north, and then over millions of years, split in two. The remainder of the supercontinent split into South America, Africa, Antarctica, Australia, and India. As he studied the coast of South America and Africa, he found that the types of rock in each place were very similar and used this evidence to support his theory. His ideas, however, were not accepted by the scientific community, and he died in 1930 having gained no support for his theory.

In later years, geologists found similar rock formations on both sides of the Atlantic Ocean. Rocks found in Brazil, Scotland, Labrador, Madagascar, India, and the Ivory Coast of Africa were alike. Fossils found on both sides of the Atlantic contained the remains of the same kinds of plants and animals that are now extinct. More importantly, however, was the discovery that the large underwater range of mountains called the 'Mid- Atlantic Ridge'. The Mid-Atlantic Ridge is located where large plates are moving away from one another creating a crack in the ocean floor. This range of mountains is constantly being built by 'magma' (hot, molten rock from the interior of the earth) which pushes itself up through the crack in the ocean floor, spreading the floor in opposite directions. Scientists then had proof to support Wegener's theory.

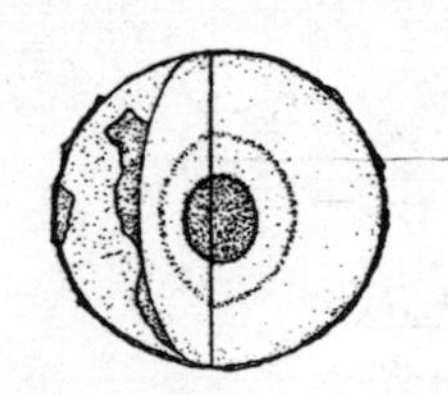

EARTH'S CRUST

In the 1970s, geologists developed a theory about the movement of the continents. This theory is known as the 'Theory of Plate Tectonics'. 'Tectonics' means building or construction. Scientists believe that the earth's crust consists of several large and small plates. Six of these large plates include all or part of a continent and some of its surrounding water. The tectonic plates all fit together on the surface of the earth like pieces of a giant jigsaw puzzle. These plates are irregular in shape, millions of square kilometers in area, and 60 to 80 km (40 to 50 mi) thick. Along with a hard upper layer of the mantle, they form the lithosphere.

Scientists believe these lithospheric plates float very slowly on the soft, molten layer of the mantle underneath the lithosphere, called the asthenosphere. Many geologists think there are strong convection currents in the mantle. These currents are formed from the heat given off by the core. They cause the asthenosphere to keep moving. The plates with continents on them travel about 2 cm (0.75 in) a year. The plates under the water shift as much as 15 cm (5 in) per year.

Geologists believe the continents have been drifting around the surface of the earth in this manner for billions of years in a process known as 'continental drift', which is responsible for many of the changes that take place on the surface of the earth. The plates are constantly moving, sliding past one another, bumping into one another and overlapping each other. Mountains and volcanoes are formed where the plates collide into one another and move away from one another, and earthquakes occur as the plates rub against on another.

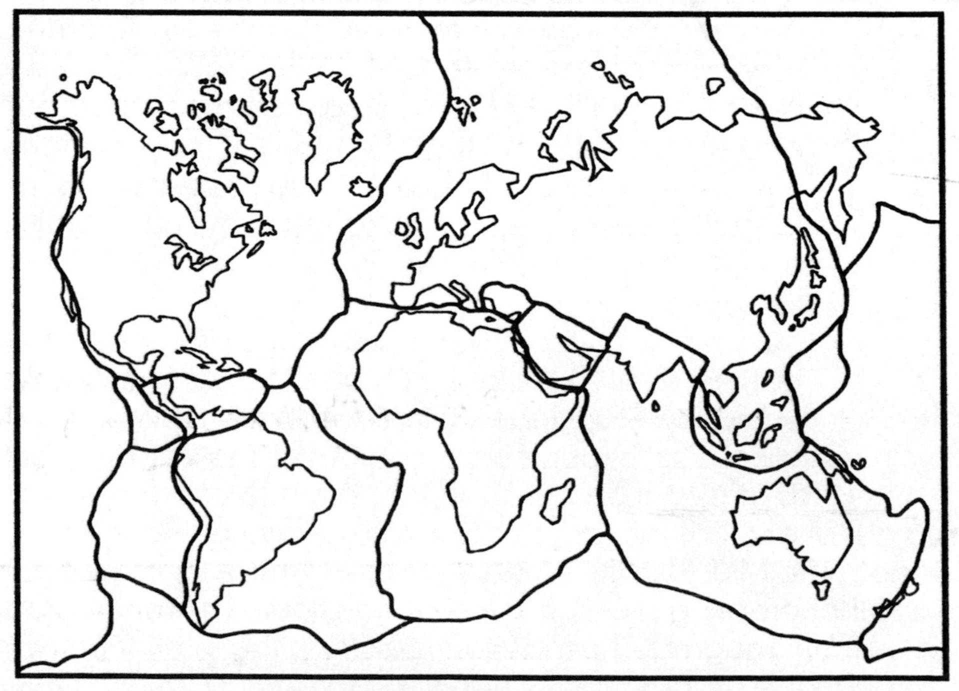

The Earth's Tectonic Plates

EARTH'S CRUST

Earth Tectonics

Info Check

1. Who was Alfred Wegener, and why was he important to the study of geology? What was his theory?

Alfred wegener was the first person to descover geology. His Theroy was all the contenets was One.

2. What made the scientific community accept Wegener's theory years later?

magma was spewing though the groundof the ocean.

3. What does the word "Pangaea" mean? all lands

4. Explain the term "continental drift".

The continents have been drifting around the surface of the Earth in this manner for billions of years in a process known as continental drift

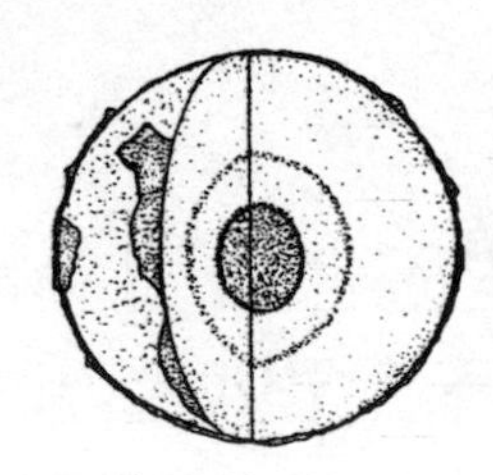

EARTH'S CRUST

The Major Tectonic Plates of the World

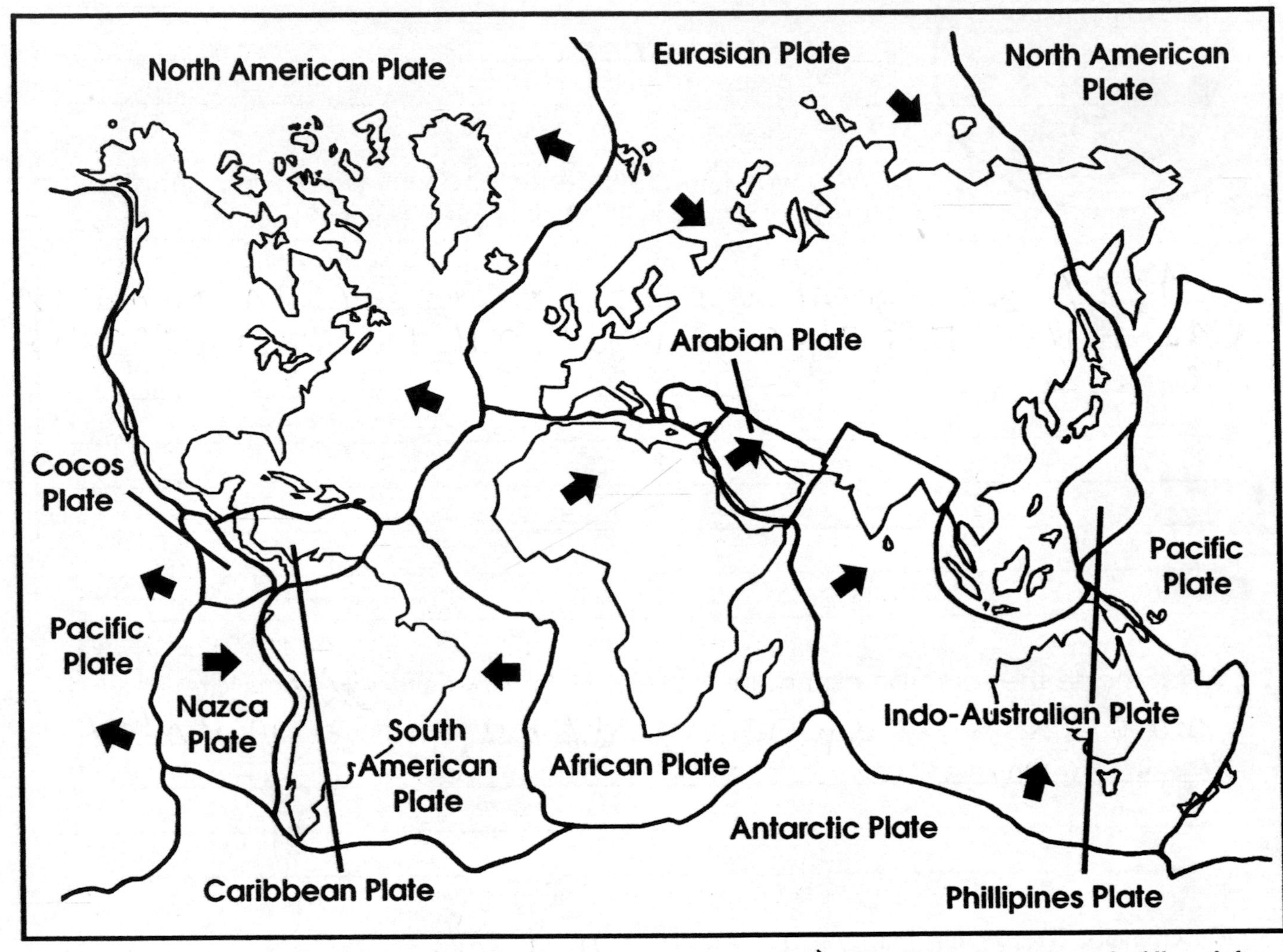

Direction of movement of the plates

5. a) Which plate does not carry a continent? pacific plate

b) Which plates are causing the volcanic action around the Iceland? North American and Eurasian plates

c) Which plates collided to form the Himalayas? ~~African and Arabian plates~~ Eurasian and Indo-Australian plate

d) Which two plates formed the rift valley that the Red Sea now occupies? African and Arabian plates

EARTH'S CRUST

6. Is the Atlantic Ocean getting wider? Explain. yes because The North American and Eurasian plates are moving away from eachother. magma's constantly oozing out of the crack between the plates forming new riges. expanding the ocean.

7. Complete the table below by naming the plate and the direction in which it is moving.

Name of Plate	Direction of Movement	Name of Plate	Direction of Movement
North American	North west	Eurasian	South West
southAmerican	west	Indo-Australian	Northwest
Pacific	Northwest	African	North East

8. The smaller plates are not labeled on the map. Using an atlas, locate the following plates and label them on your map. If possible, find the direction in which they are moving.

   a) Cocos Plate b) Caribbean Plate c) Philippines Plate

9. Using the map below draw the Pacific Plate.

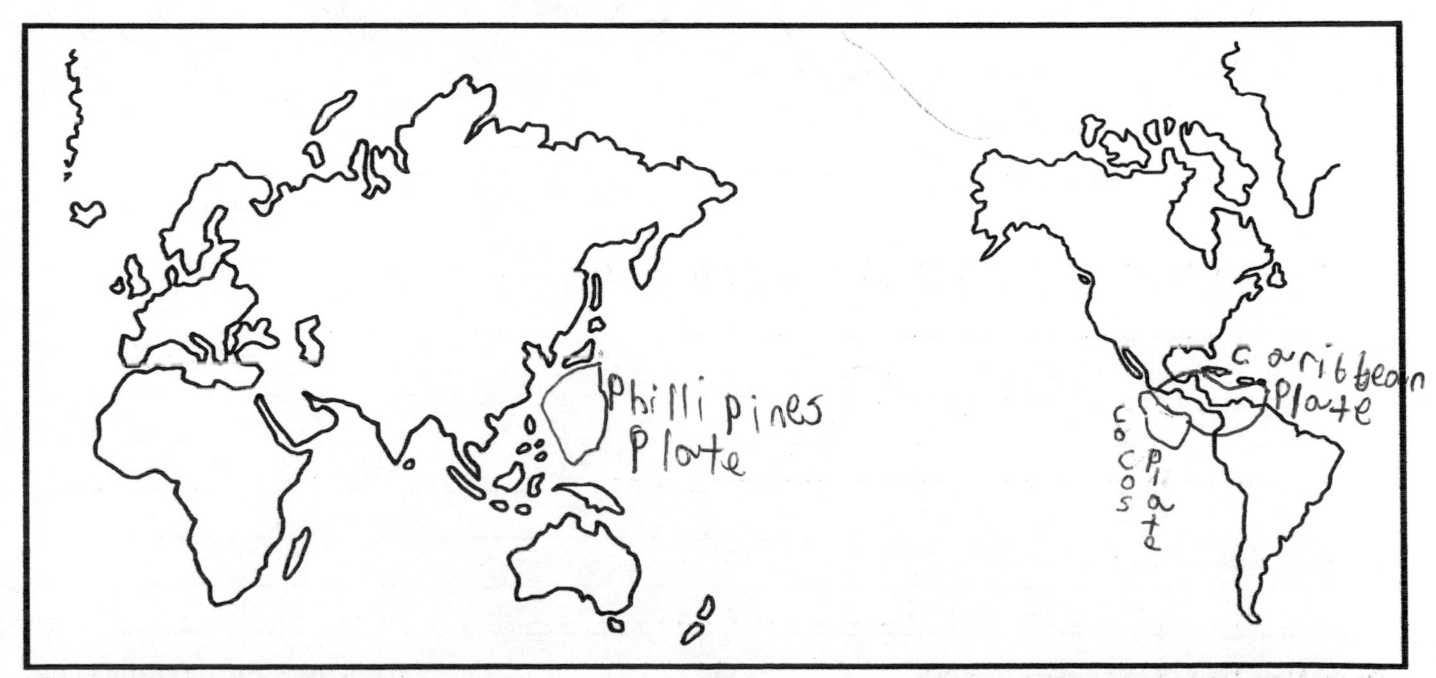

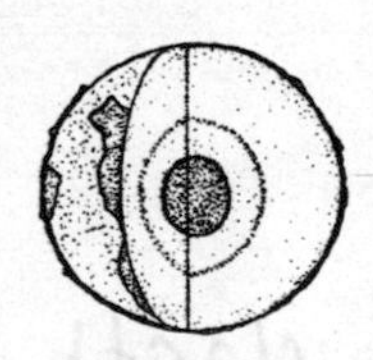

EARTH'S CRUST

10. The maps below show how the continents have moved over the past 200 million years. Try to identify the continents on each map. Some believe the continents will form a 'supercontinent' again.

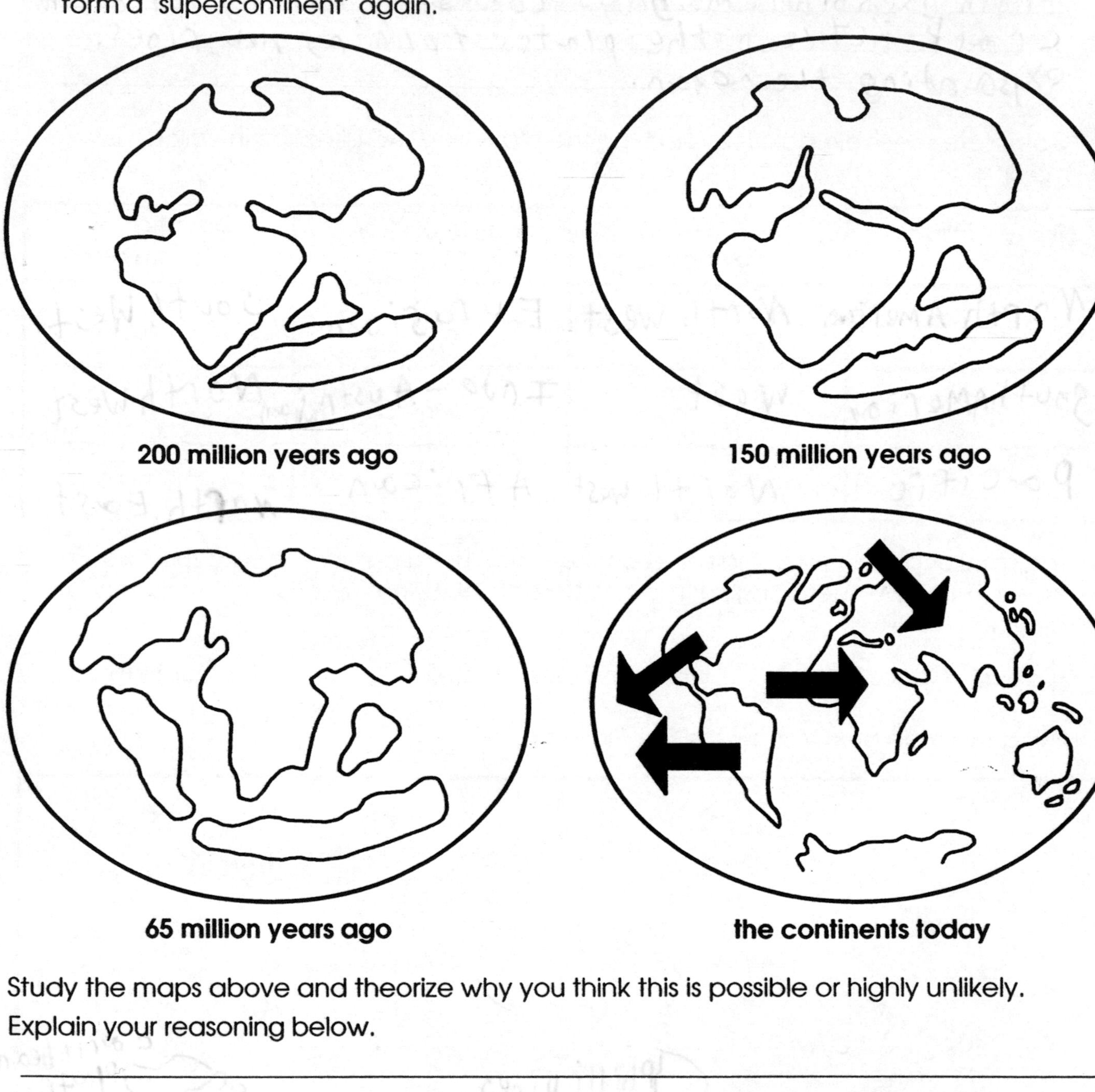

Study the maps above and theorize why you think this is possible or highly unlikely. Explain your reasoning below.

EARTH'S CRUST

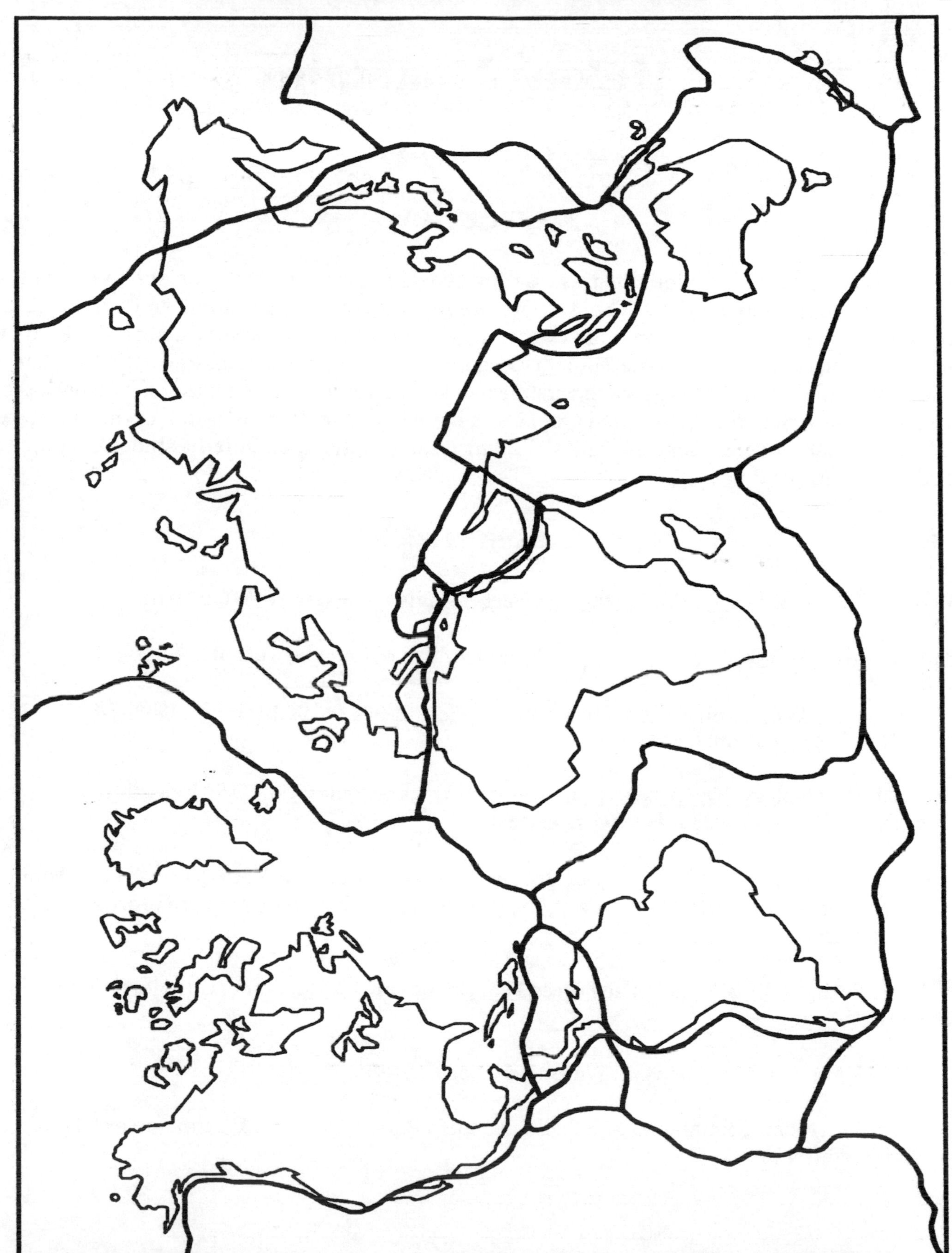

The Major Tectonic Plates of the World

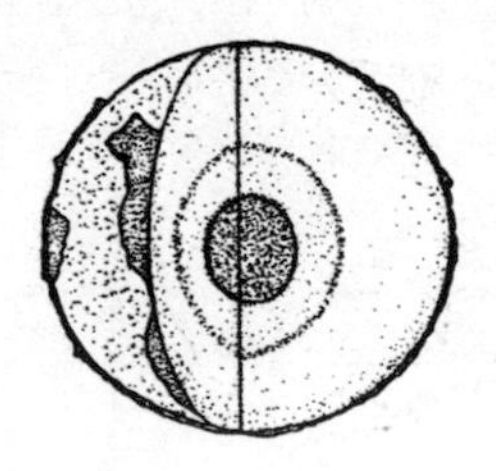

EARTH'S CRUST

Making Mountains

Teacher Input

Overview

This component examines the processes involved in mountain formation and in the folding and faulting of the earth's crust. The students will find the concepts of folding and faulting easier to understand if allowed time to simulate the processes with simple materials. Most books about the earth's surface and mountains contain ideas for simple demonstrations and activities that can be easily carried out in the classroom with inexpensive materials. One suggestion is to have the students' research and work in small groups to devise their own demonstration of the processes. This component involves concepts and skills which can be integrated into the students' course of study in geography.

Resources

McConnell, Anita. The World Beneath Us. Facts on File Inc.; New York, ©1985.

Parker, Steve. The Earth and How it Works. Macmillan of Canada; Toronto, ©1989.

Parker, Steve. The Marshall Cavendish Science Project Book of the Earth. Marshall Cavendish Pub.; New York, ©1986.

Braus, Judy. Geology: The Active Earth. National Wildlife Federation; Washington D.C., ©1988. (this is an excellent teacher resource)

Farndon, John. How the Earth Works. Reader's Digest Assoc.; New York, ©1992. (this book provides a wealth of simple student activities which clearly demonstrate earth processes; highly recommended)

Hehner, Barbara. Blue Planet: The Forces That Shape Our World. Somerville House Pub.; Toronto, ©1992.

Bramwell, Martyn. Mountains. F. Watts; New York, ©1986.

William, Lawrence. Mountains. Marshall Cavendish Pub.; New York, ©1990. (an excellent student resource)

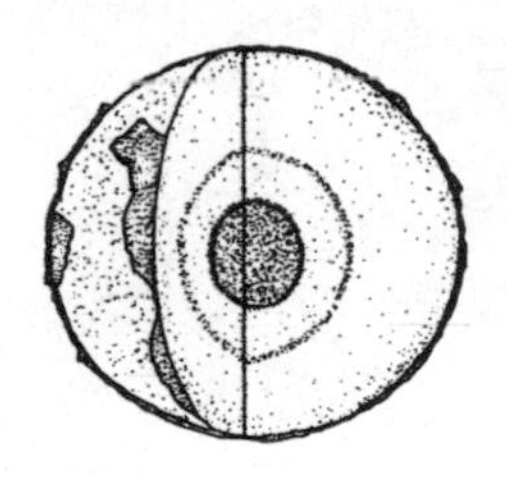

EARTH'S CRUST

Making Mountains

Answers

Info Check: ***(page 40)***

1. A mountain is an area of high land or rock which rises above the surrounding lowlands.
2. Mountains affect the wind, temperature, and water supply of an area, and thus control what will grow and the animals that can live there.
3.

Mountain Range	Continent
Himalayas	Eurasia
Andes	South America
Rockies	North America
Alps	Eurasia

4. Mountains are formed as lithospheric plates collide with one another. Pressure causes the rock to fold or wrinkle, dome or break. If magma finds it way to the surface through an opening created by the pressure, a volcanic mountain is formed.
5. Rockies – fold mountains
6. Fault – a crack in the earth, may be small or several hundreds of kilometers long, formed when the rocks of the earth's crust break, a very unstable area.
7. Oceanic plates are much heavier than continental plates because the rock from which they are formed is much denser.
8. As the thin oceanic plate collides with the thicker, but lighter, continental plate, the oceanic plate is subducted down under the continental plate. The oceanic plate begins to melt as it reaches the hotter areas of the asthenosphere. Magma is then forced up through openings to the earth's crust forming volcanic mountains.
9. The Mid-Atlantic Ridge is an underwater mountain range extending from Iceland to Antarctica. It is constantly being formed by magma oozing up through a large crack, in the ocean floor where plates are moving apart.
10. As the plates move away form one another, magma finds it way through the cracks created by the plates and reaches the surface of the ocean floor. As the magma flows out of the crack, it forms ridges which spread and cause the ocean floor to grow wider.
11. The youngest rocks in the ridge are those closest to the crack as this is where new magma is constantly forming the ridge.

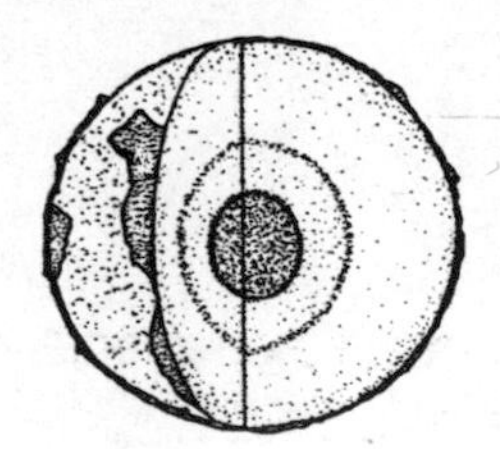

EARTH'S CRUST

Making Mountains

Information Card #4

Most mountains are part of long chains that run for hundreds of kilometers across the surface of the earth. There are four great ranges of really high mountains on the surface of the earth: the Himalayas, the Andes, the Rockies and the Alps. The highest mountains in the world are the Himalayas. Mountains affect the wind, temperature and water supply of huge areas and thus control what can be grown in certain areas of the world. Mountain ranges also control the animal life living in a particular region.

By studying the structure of mountain ranges, geologists have discovered how the powerful forces inside the earth have been shaping the face of our planet for millions of years. These pressures shape the continents by causing earthquakes and volcanoes and by building mountains. Geologists have discovered that mountains are formed where the crust of the earth is distributed by the great pressure inside the earth. All over the world, mountains are being formed. Many mountain ranges contain active volcanoes, while others are constantly shaken by earthquakes.

Geologists divide mountains into four main types: 'fold' mountains, 'dome' mountains, 'block fault' mountains, and 'volcanic' mountains. As the large plates of the earth drift on the molten layer of rock beneath the crust, the edges of the lithospheric plates sometimes collide with one another and place great pressure on the rocks. If rocks are under pressure for a long period of time, they will slowly bend or fold like the wrinkles made in a carpet when heavy furniture is dragged over it. When rock is placed under great pressure, it becomes hot. It might then bend upwards forming a dome or it might fold, creating waves in the rock, and creating mountains and valleys. When plates collide and the enormous pressure squeezes the horizontal rocks, causing them the wrinkle or fold, fold mountains are formed. All of the world's greatest mountain ranges, including the Andes, Rockies, Alps, and Himalayas, have been folded during the crashing together of two tectonic plates. When the Indo-Australian plate, carrying India, collided with the Eurasian plate, the Himalayas were created.

If the pressure on rock is too great or too sudden, the rock will break. When rock breaks, 'faults' or large cracks are created in the earth's crust. Faults may be small or they may be hundreds of kilometers long. Some mountains are formed when blocks of

EARTH'S CRUST

land slide up or down along fault lines in the earth's crust. Faults are very unstable areas and there are frequent earthquakes and sometimes volcanic activity along fault lines. The famous San Andreas Fault, which runs through much of California for nearly 1 000 km (620 mi) is located where the Pacific and North American plates slide past each other. In 1906 a great earthquake happened along this fault in San Francisco. The land beside the fault moved 6 m (20 ft)! Scientists predict there will be a major earthquake in this part of the world in the next few years.

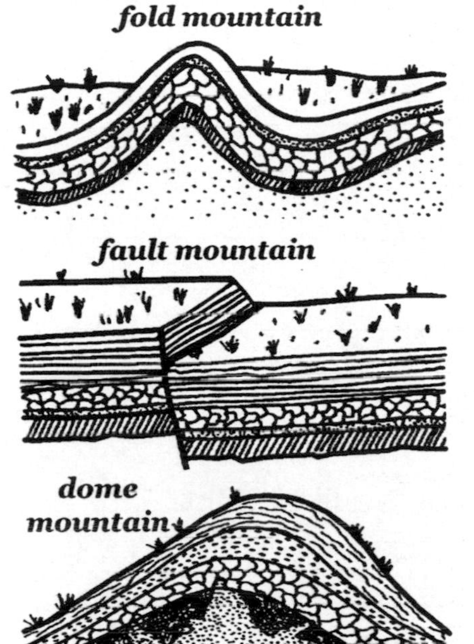

The bending and folding of rock usually takes millions of years. However, a fault or crack in the earth can appear very suddenly during a violent earthquake. Other new mountains may form in a matter of days as a volcano erupts from the earth. Almost all volcanoes in the world erupt along the borders of two plates.

Ocean plates are much heavier then continental plates (plates carrying continents) because the rock of which they are formed is much denser. When a continental plate and an ocean plate collide, the heavier oceanic plate is forced downward or 'subducted' under the lighter continental plate. The edge of the continental plate is crumpled as the oceanic plate slides down under it and a mountain range is formed along the margin of the upper (continental) plate. This is how the Andes mountains were formed! As the oceanic plate, the subducted plate, is forced under into the hotter regions of the mantle, part of it begins to melt. The melted rock is less dense than the rock of the mantle and starts to move upward. It erupts through volcanoes that have been formed on the upper plate.

Mountains are also formed as tectonic plates move away from one another. Areas where tectonic plates are moving away from one another are called 'spreading zones'. These zones are usually found beneath the ocean. Sometimes the tips of mountains rise out of the water creating islands. As the plates move apart, molten rock, called 'magma', rises up from the earth's mantle and fills in the 'rift' that is formed as the plates move apart. As the magma hardens, it forms a mountain ridge. On top of the mountain ridge is a 'rift valley'. The Red Sea occupies a rift valley.

This spreading on the ocean floors is happening in all the world's major oceans. The greatest mountain range in the world is a 60 000 km (36 000 mi) chain of mountains which form great winding paths around the world - under the oceans! A 20 000 km (12 000 mi) portion of the range is called the Mid-Atlantic Ridge and it extends from Iceland almost to Antarctica. Magma is constantly oozing out of this ridge which separates the North American plate from the Eurasian plate. As the Mid-Atlantic Ridge grows, the Atlantic Ocean continues to get wider.

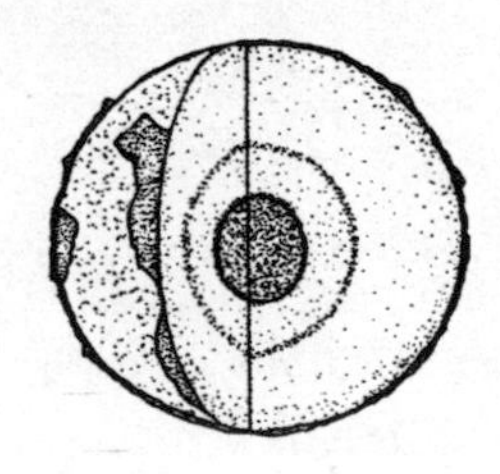

EARTH'S CRUST

Making Mountains

Info Check

1. What is a mountain? ____

2. How do mountains affect life on earth? ____

3. Name the four highest mountain ranges on the surface of the earth and the continents on which they are located.

Mountain Range	Continent

4. Explain how mountains are formed.

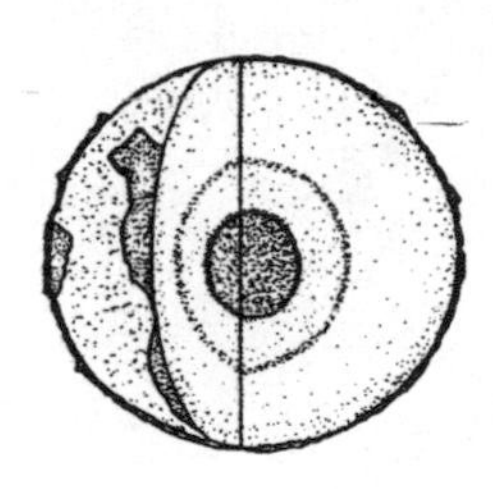

EARTH'S CRUST

5. What type of mountains are the Rockies? ______________________________

6. Explain the term "fault". ______________________________________

____

____

____

7. What major difference is there between an oceanic plate and a continental plate?

____

____

____

____

____

8. The diagram below illustrates the process of subduction. Study the diagram and then using the proper vocabulary, write an explanation of that is happening.

____

____

____

____

____

____

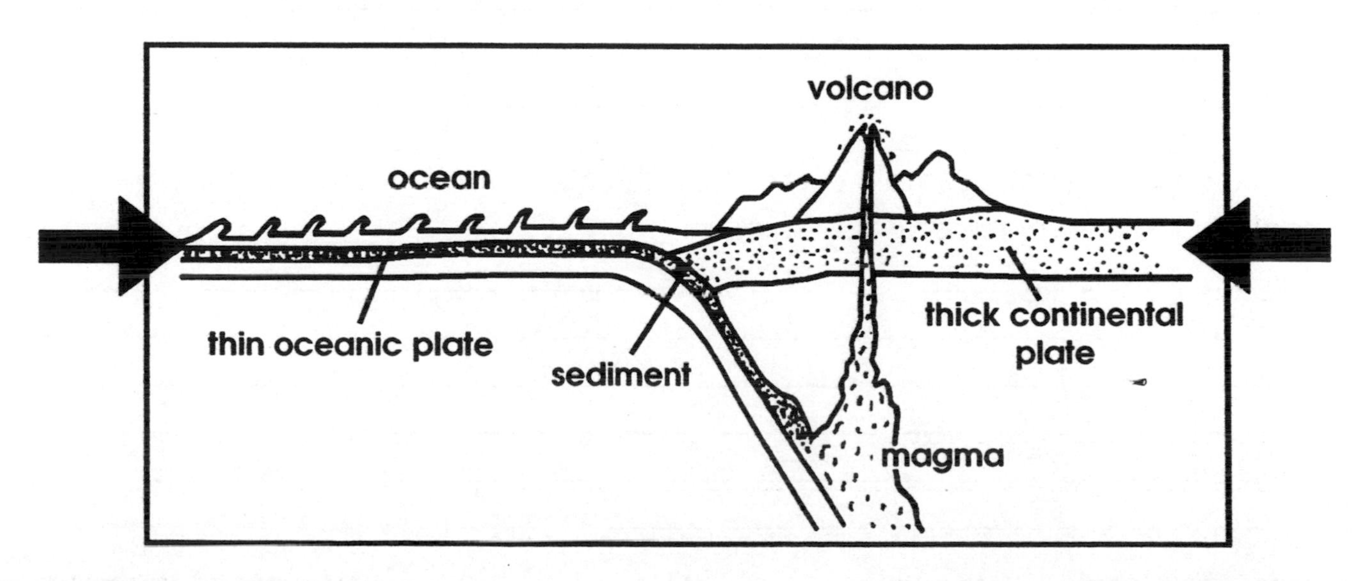

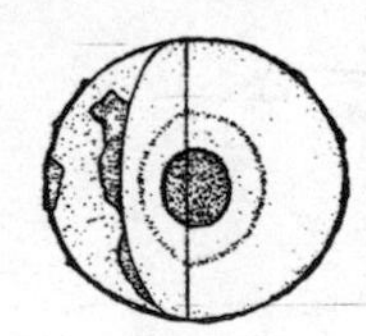

EARTH'S CRUST

9. What is the Mid-Atlantic Ridge? ______________________________

____

____

____

10. Study the diagram carefully and then explain how the Mid-Atlantic Ridge is formed.

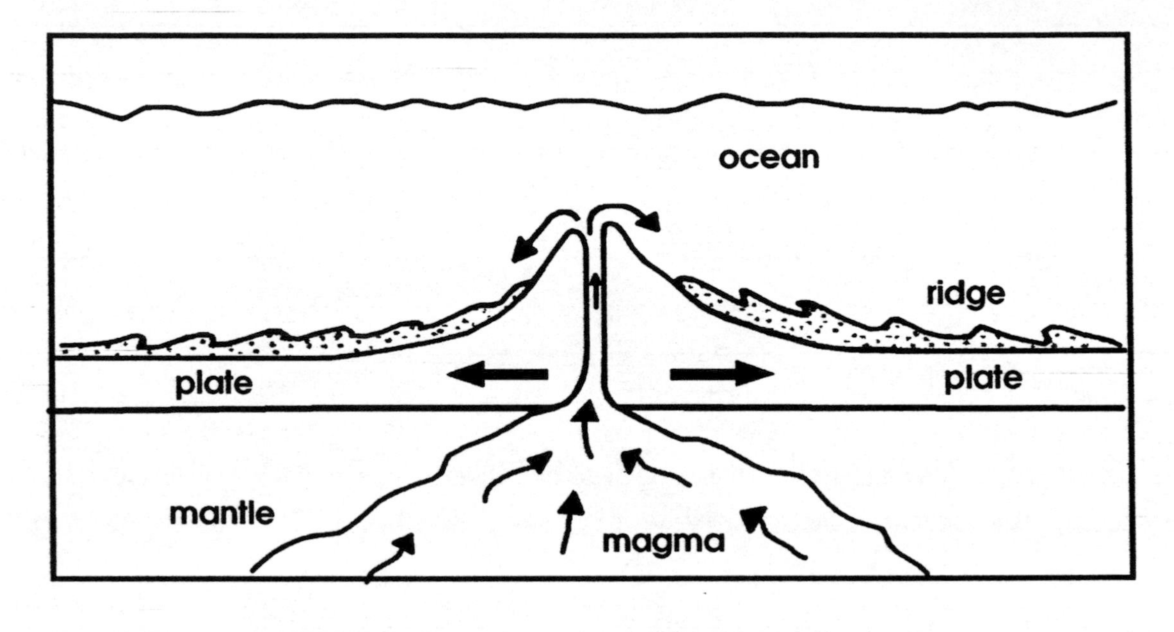

____

____

____

____

____

____

____

11. If you could collect a sample of rock from the Mid-Atlantic Ridge, where would you look to find the youngest rocks? Explain. ______________________________

____

____

____

____

____

____

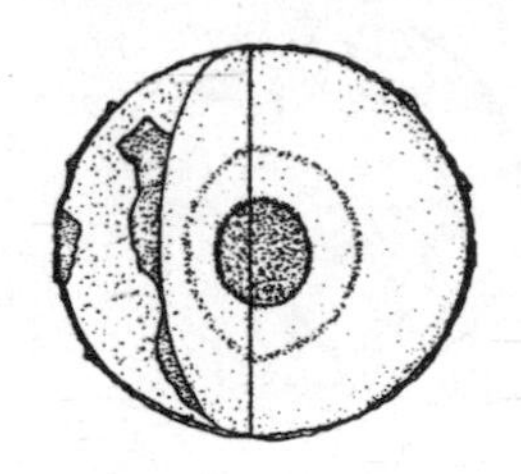

EARTH'S CRUST

Earthquakes

Teacher Input

Overview

This component examines the phenomenon of earthquakes. The students will gain an understanding of the forces which cause earthquakes by relating their knowledge of plate tectonics to the earthquake regions of the world. They are familiarized with the terminology associated with earthquakes as they learn how earthquakes are recorded and measured. An important part of their study of earthquakes should involve an understanding of the technology used by scientists to monitor and predict earthquakes. Students will design and build their own seismometer as part of this component, however, the activity could include other projects such as designing earthquake-proof buildings. Other activities could require students to access electronic encyclopedias and web sites to gather up-to-date information about earthquakes and around the world. This component lends itself to the making of charts, graphs, tables, etc. and could be integrated with data management activities in Mathematics.

Resources

Farndon, John. How the Earth Works. Reader's Digest Assoc.; New York, ©1992.

Rogers, Daniel. Earthquakes. Raintree Steck-Vaughin; Texas, ©1999.

Nicolson, Cynthia Pratt. Earthdance. Kids Can Press; Toronto, ©1994.

Nixon, Hershell. Earthquakes: Nature in Motion. Dodd Mead; New York, ©1981.

Moores, Eldridge. Volcanoes and Earthquakes. Time-Life Books; Alexandria Va., ©1995.

Vrbova, Zuza. Volcanoes and Earthquakes. Eagle Books Ltd.; New Jersey, ©1990.

Walker, Sally M. Earthquakes. Carolrhoda Books; Minn., ©1996.

Dudman, John. Earthquake. Wayland Pub.; England, ©1992.

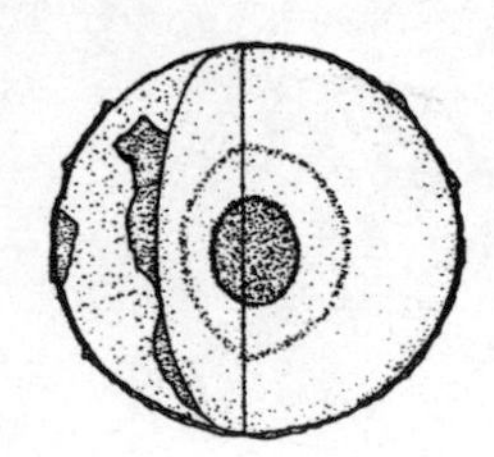

EARTH'S CRUST

Earthquakes

Answers

<u>Info Check</u>: ***(page 47)***

1. **a)** ***Magnitude*** – How much energy is given off by the earthquake, measured by the size of the seismic waves, measured on the Richter Scale.
   b) ***Intensity*** – A measure of how badly the earthquake shakes people and objects and the damage it causes to buildings, measured on the Mercalli Scale.
   c) Seismograph – An instrument for measuring the size of seismic waves.
   d) ***Tremor*** – A slight shaking of the earth, can sometimes be barely felt, causes no damage, often warns earthquakes.
2. The Richter Scale gives each earthquake a number from one to ten based on how much the ground shook. A one on the scale is the mildest quake.
3. Animals are often sensitive to even the slightest tremors before an earthquake and will clear buildings or show signs of restlessness, etc.
4. Tidal waves or tsunamis, Mudslides, avalanches
5. Diagrams may vary.
6. **a)** ***Fault line*** – The border between two plates that are grinding and pushing against one another.
   b) ***Focus*** – The point beneath the rock's surface where the rock breaks.
   c) ***Epicenter*** – The spot on the surface of the earth directly above the focus.
7. Ring of Fire – Follows the coast line of North America and China, Most Earthquakes and volcanoes in this area.

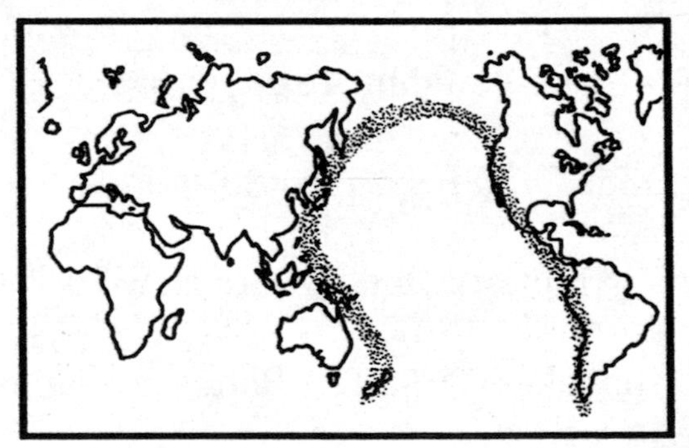

<u>Research Challenge</u>: ***(page 50)***

This is a picture of the ancient Chinese seismometer.
It can be found in many books about earthquakes.

<u>Technology Challenge</u>: ***(page 51)***

This is a challenging technology activity. Students will have fun trying to make their own seismometer.

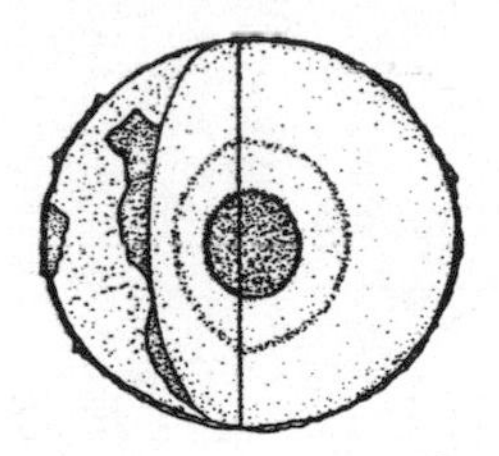

EARTH'S CRUST

Earthquakes

Information Card #5

The earth's crust is constantly on the move. Most of the movements are slow and changes to the earth's surface are gradual. Sometimes, however, there are sudden and violent movements. Some of these violent movements cause earthquakes. The earth heaves and shakes and even splits open causing great terror and damage. Houses, schools and factories may topple. Bridges may snap in two and roads may be gobbled up by the earth. Power and gas lines may break causing great fires. Thousands of people may lose their lives.

Earthquakes may take place anywhere on the earth but are likely to happen in certain parts of the word more than others. Many earthquakes take place under the sea and nine out of ten earthquakes take place along fault lines, the borders between plates that are grinding and pushing against one another. Although faults may be hundreds of kilometers long, earthquakes take place along a short section of the fault, only a few kilometers long. More than twenty different plate edges are known to be earthquake zones. The most active earthquake area is the edge of the Pacific Plate. This plate follows the coastline of North and South America and China and is known as the "Ring of Fire" due to the many earthquakes and volcanoes along its edge.

The famous San Andreas fault forms part of the border between the North American plate and the Pacific plate. The Pacific plate, which floats in a northwestward direction, scrapes past the North American plate. Each time the plates break free of each other there is an earthquake. There have been many major quakes along the San Andreas fault in the last hundred years, including the great San Francisco earthquake in 1906.

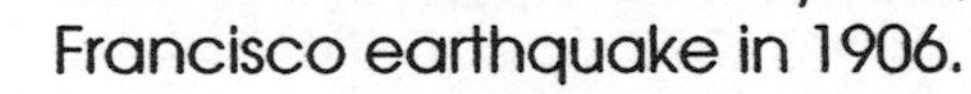

Scientists estimate there is at least one earthquake somewhere in the world everyday. As the great lithospheric plates move about the surface of the earth, they often scrape and slide against one another. Sometimes they do not slide one another smoothly but get snagged against one another. The tremendous pressure builds up until eventually the rocks break away with such tremendous force that an earthquake occurs. The tremors caused by some earthquakes can barely be felt. Other earthquakes cause major disasters.

Earthquakes vary greatly in strength which is measured in terms of 'magnitude' and 'intensity'. The magnitude of an earthquake refers to the size of the seismic waves and is measured on the Richter Scale using a instrument called a 'seismograph'. 'Seismos' is the Greek word meaning 'to shake'. The Richter Scale gives each earthquake a number based on how much the ground shook. On the

EARTH'S CRUST

Richter Scale, a measurement of one is a very mild quake, and ten is the most violent. Any quake over seven is a very destructive quake.

When measuring an earthquake, the magnitude, or how much energy is given off, is not determind by how much damage is caused. Sometimes more damage is done by the fires that start from the earthquake than the actual earthquake itself. The largest quake ever measured on the Ritcher Scale had a magnitude of about 8.9. The great earthquake in Anchorage, Alaska was 8.6 on the Richter Scale. The intensity of an earthquake is a measure of how badly the earthquake shakes people and objects, and the damage it causes to buildings. It is measured on the 'Mercalli Intensity Scale'.

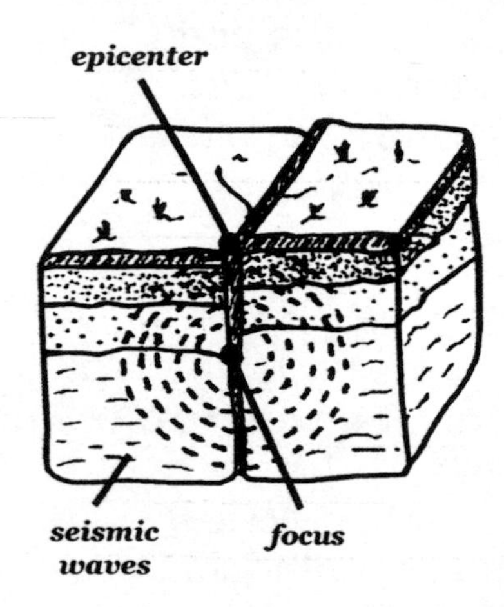

During an earthquake, energy is released in the form of waves from a point called the 'focus'. This point is where the rock first breaks and can be up to 700 km (450 mi) beneath the surface. The seismic waves radiate from the focus causing the ground to vibrate. There are several kinds of seismic waves and they travel at different speeds depending of the type of rock they are traveling through. Waves are emitted in all directions through the earth. They travel up, down and sideways. By receiving and measuring the different types of waves coming from the focus, seismologists can tell where the quake occurred, the time it occurred, and its magnitude.

Along with starting fires, earthquakes can set off avalanches, landslides and mudslides as tremendous amounts of snow, ice, mud and rock are sometimes loosened by the force of the quake. An earthquake or volcanic eruption under the ocean can cause a huge wave called a "tsunami" or "tidal wave" which can travel up to 800 km/ hour (500 mph). A tsunami can reach heights of 30 m (100 ft) causing terrible damage as it crashes into shore. Most tidal waves occur in the Pacific ocean where they are set off by underwater quakes and eruptions.

Scientists are always looking for ways to predict major earthquakes, but are not always successful. Many earthquakes are recorded by seismographs every day in stations all around the world. Some areas of the world are constantly monitored for earthquakes. Seismographs and other special equipment can detect small tremors below the surface of the earth. Seismologists time the seismic waves and are then able to tell where the 'epicenter' of the earthquake is located. The epicenter is the point on the surface of the earth directly above the focus of the quake. Satellites, thousands of kilometers above the earth, record the tiniest movement in the earth's plates.

Animals often give warning signs of earthquakes. It has been noticed that animals get very restless and often leave an area when an earthquake is coming! Earthquakes, however, can happen without any warning, and so scientists continue to study and improve their knowledge of earthquakes, and preventive measures are taken to help reduce damage and the loss of life in earthquake zones. Today, buildings are designed and built to withstand even some of the biggest tremors.

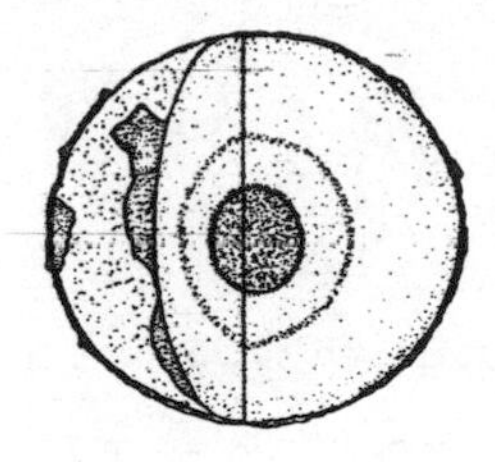

EARTH'S CRUST

Earthquakes

Info Check

1. Explain the following terms:

   a) magnitude: ______________________________

   b) intensity: ______________________________

   c) seismograph: ______________________________

   d) tremor: ______________________________

2. What is the Richter Scale? ______________________________

3. How are animals sometimes useful in earthquake zones? ______________________________

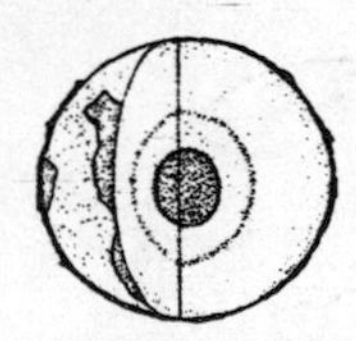

EARTH'S CRUST

4. Along with the earthquake, what other natural occurrences can cause serious damage?

____
____
____
____
____

5. Draw a diagram of an earthquake which shows the following: earth's crust, seismic waves, focus, epicenter. Label your diagram.

6. Describe the following:

a) fault line: ____
____
____

b) focus: ____
____
____

c) epicenter: ____
____
____

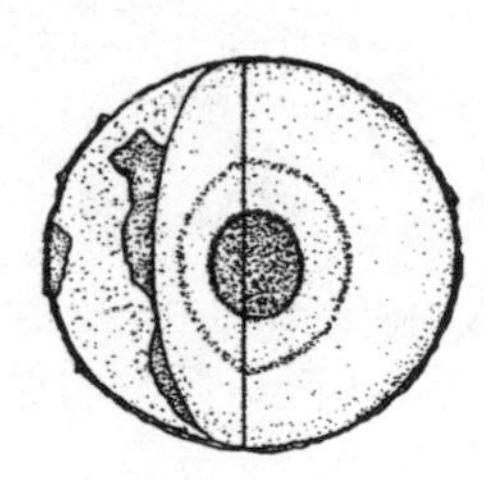

EARTH'S CRUST

7. What is the "Ring of Fire"? ____

____

____

____

____

____

____

____

____

8. On the map below, label the following: **the continents**
   the ocean
   the Pacific Plate
   the 'Ring of Fire'

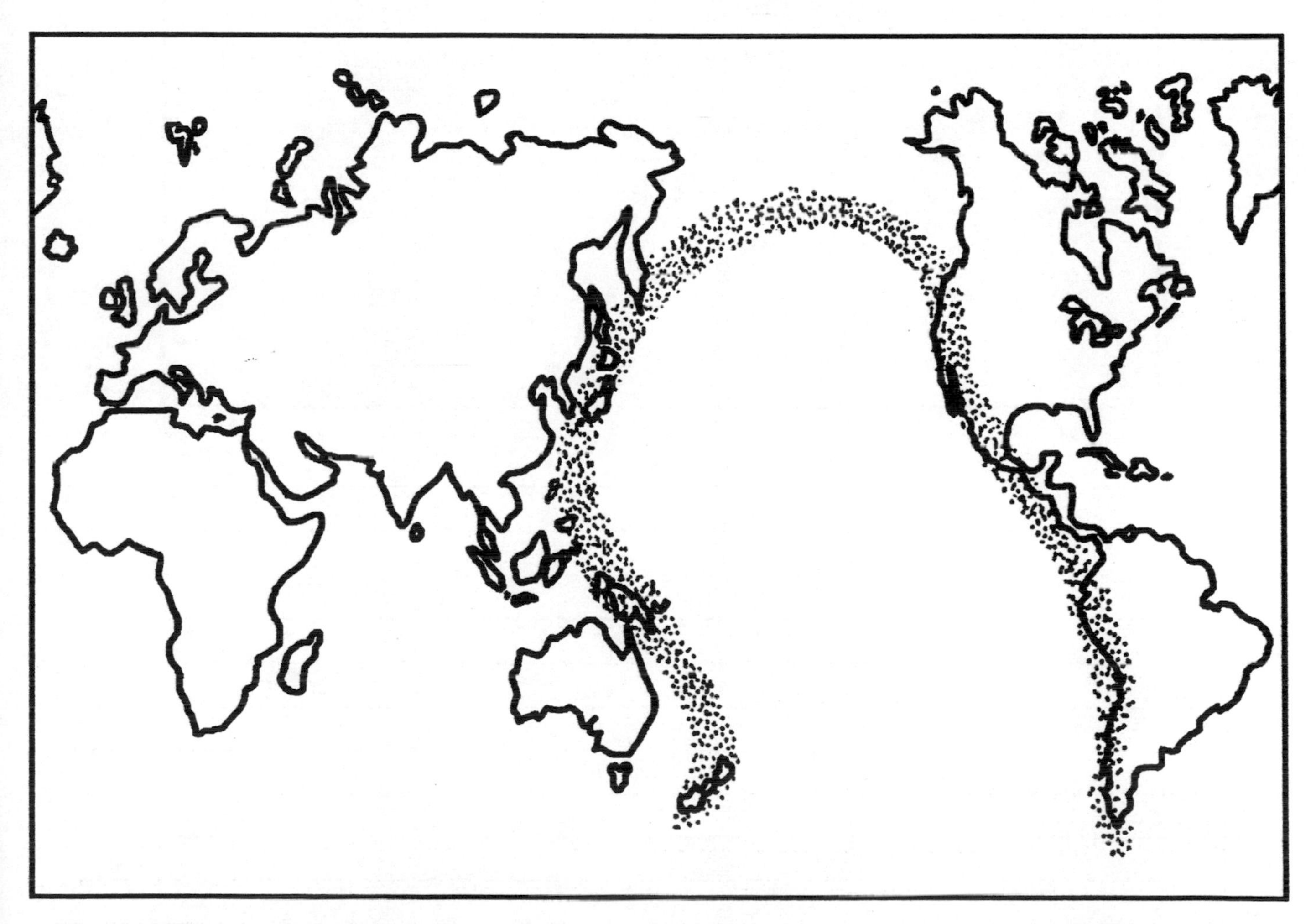

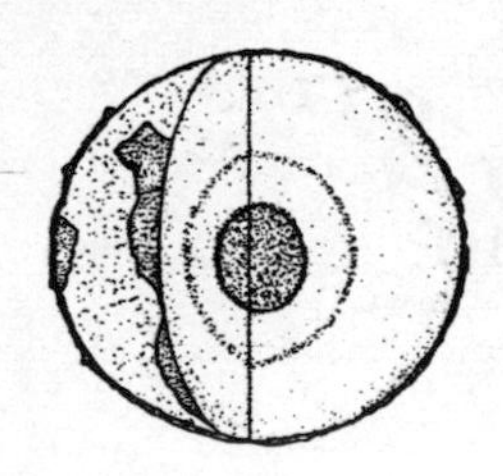

EARTH'S CRUST

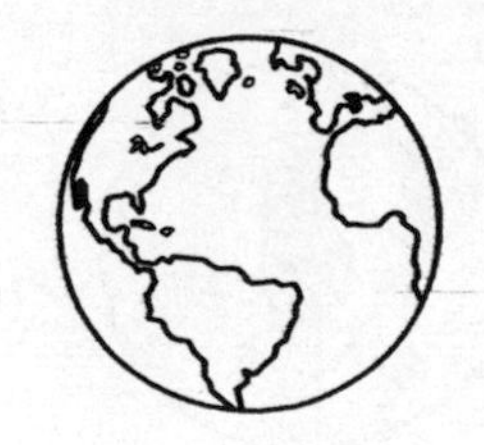

Earthquakes

Research Challenge

A seismometer is a device used to register an earthquake. The ancient Chinese developed one of the earliest seismometers. Do some research to find a picture of this seismometer. Draw a picture of it in the box below, and explain how it worked.

Hint: The design includes two different animals: one mythical and one real.

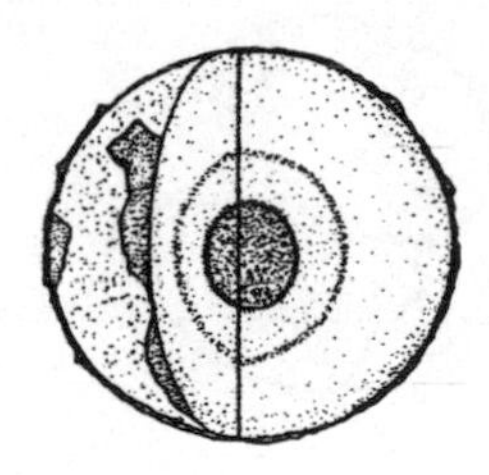

EARTH'S CRUST

Earthquakes

Technology Challenge

Make a Seismometer

How it works: ____

____

____

____

____

____

Diagram	Materials Used

Problems I experienced: ____

____

____

____

I think my seismometer____

____

____

____

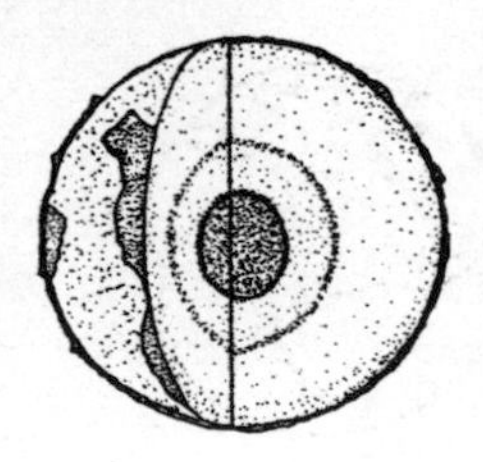

EARTH'S CRUST

Volcanoes

Teacher Input

Overview

This component explores the formation of volcanoes. Students will learn how and where volcanoes are most likely to occur, and relate their findings to their knowledge of plate tectonics, continental drift, and the composition of the earth's interior. They will learn several geological terms related to volcanoes. This component can be extended by having the students access web sites on current volcanic activity around the world. Language activities could involve an exploration of the ancient myths surrounding volcanoes.

Resources

McConnell, Anita. The World Beneath Us. Facts on File Inc.; New York, ©1985.

Parker, Steve. The Earth and How it Works. MacMillan of Canada; Toronto, ©1989.

Parker, Steve. The Marshal Cavendish Science Project Book of the Earth. Marshall Cavendish Pub.; New York, ©1986.

Farndon, John. How the Earth Works. Reader's Digest Assoc.; New York, ©1992.

Markle, Sandra. Digging Deeper. Lothrop, Lee and Shepard Books; New York, ©1987.

Nicolson, Cynthia Pratt. Earthdance. Kids Can Press; Toronto, ©1994.

Simon, Seymour. Volcanoes. Morrow Junior Books; New York, ©1988.

Moores, Eldridge. Volcanoes and Earthquakes. Eagle Books Ltd.; New Jersey, ©1990.

Clarke, Penny. Volcanoes. F. Watts; New York, ©1998.

*National Geographic has produced an excellent video about volcanoes.

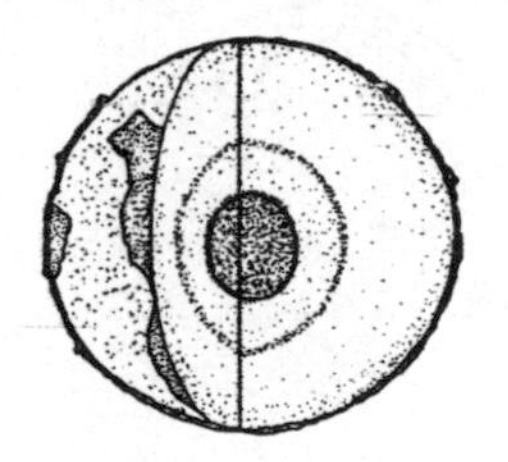

EARTH'S CRUST

Volcanoes

Answers

<u>**Info Check**</u>**:** ***(page 56)***

1. **a)** ***Active volcano*** – Has steam or gases coming from it and when it erupts, it spews out lava and ash.
   b) ***Dormant volcano*** – Not active now, but may become active in the future.
   c) ***Extinct volcano*** – Has not shown any activity for so long that scientists believe it is not likely to become active again.
2. Answers may vary.
3. Geothermal energy is produced from water that has been heated by hot rock under the surface of the earth.

4.

a	Sicily	**h**	Paricutin
b	The Pacific Plate	**f**	hot spot
c	Washington	**i**	volcano belt
d	Iceland	**d**	geothermal energy
e	North Atlantic Ocean	**j**	hot spring
f	Hawaiian Islands	**g**	geyser
g	Yellowstone Park	**a**	Mt. Etna
h	Mexico	**b**	volcano belt
i	Mediterranean Sea	**e**	Surtsey
j	New Zealand	**c**	Mount St. Helens

5. The Hawaiian Islands were formed over hot spots. A hot spot is usually found in the middle of a plate where magma has risen through the mantle and melted a hole through the earth's crust forming a volcano.

6. Lava is magma that has reached the earth's surface.

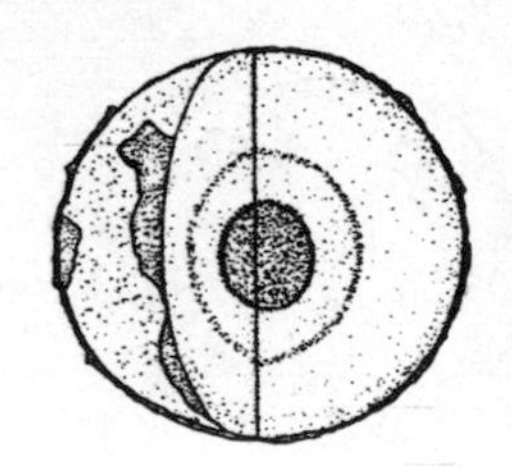

EARTH'S CRUST

Volcanoes

Information Card #6

The word "volcano" comes from the ancient Latin name Vulcanus. Valcanus (today called Vulcano) is an island north of Sicily which the Romans believed was the home of their god of fire, Vulcan. Vulcano is a volcanic island which, like all volcanoes, has been built up of magma form inside the earth. Many of the earth's islands, mountains and plains have been shaped by volcanoes.

When magma pushes its way up through the cracks or weak spots in the earth's surface, it forms a volcano. A volcano can be a hole in the ground that the lava comes up through, or it can be a hill or mountain formed by the lava. The magma may ooze out of the earth and flow gently over the crust, or it may shoot out of the earth in a violent explosion of steam and gases. These are the most spectacular types of eruptions. Hot molten rock and ash sometimes shoot many kilometers into the air.

An 'active' volcano has steam or gas coming from it, and when it erupts, it spews out lava and ash. A volcano which is not active now but may become active in the future is said to be 'dormant' or 'sleeping'. An extinct volcano is one which has not shown any activity in such a long time that scientists believe it is not likely to become active again. Most volcanoes occur along two 'volcano belts'. The biggest belt is the Ring of Fire which is located along the edges of the Pacific plate. The Ring of Fire forms an irregular circle around the Pacific Ocean. Most volcanoes and earthquakes occur along the edges of the Pacific plate as it slides or scrapes past other plates. The smaller volcano belt is located along the northern edge of the Mediterranean Sea.

Volcanoes are made in different ways. They can be formed where plates collide into one another in 'subduction zones'. As the plates rub against one another, one plate sometimes slips under the other and is pushed down or subducted into the earth. As this plate is pushed down, the enormous heat inside the earth melts part of the plate, changing it into magma. S ome of this magma may then push its way up through the plate above, forming a hole, or volcano, through which magma escapes. This type of magma is usually very thick and sticky, and when it is mixed with steam and gases, it explodes out of the volcano with great force. A volcano that forms this way is called a 'stratovolcano'. Most of the volcanoes in the world are stratovolcanoes.

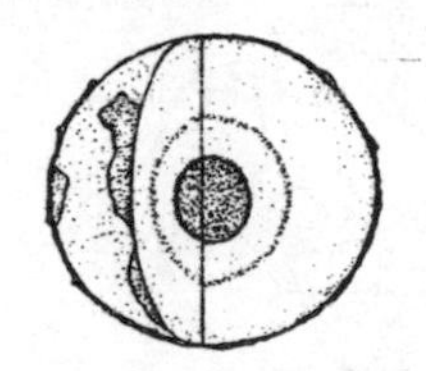

EARTH'S CRUST

Another type of volcano, called a 'shield' volcano, is formed in the middle of a plate above a source of hot magma called a 'hot spot'. Hot spots are located where magma has risen through the magma and melted a hole in the earth's crust. As the magma flows out of the opening in the earth's crust it is called 'lava'. Lava from shield volcanoes is usually thin and runs out of the volcano like a river. A hot spot stays still but the tectonic plate keeps moving. As the plate moves, volcanoes that were located on hot spots become dormant and new volcanoes are formed in a different location. Over many millions of years, chains of volcanic islands such as the Hawaiian Islands are formed.

The volcanoes in the Hawaiian Islands are shield volcanoes found in the middle of the Pacific plate. The largest Hawaiian volcano is Mauna Loa which forms the island of Hawaii. It is an active volcano and erupts every few years.

In the middle of the North Atlantic Ocean, two plates are slowly moving apart and hot magma is pushed up between them forming a chain of underwater volcanoes. Some of the underwater volcanoes are so high that they stick up out of the ocean as islands. Iceland is one of these islands. In 1963, an undersea volcano exploded in this area and formed a new island named Surtsey.

Even though a volcano may have stopped erupting, rock and magma chambers below may remain for thousands of years. Sometimes water will circulate below the ground and come into contact with this hot rock. As the hot water rises to the surface of the earth it forms what is called a 'hot spring'. There are three areas in the world famous for their hot springs. These are Iceland, Yellowstone Park, U.S.A., and North Island, New Zealand. The temperature of hot springs varies from warm to extremely hot. 'Geysers' are hot springs from which fountains of hot water and steam shoot into the air. Energy can be produced from hot springs and is called 'geothermal energy'. Iceland, which lies across two of the earth's plates, has many volcanoes and uses geothermal energy (the heat from the hot springs) to heat homes.

Scientists use special instruments to help them predict volcanic eruptions by measuring the heat flow beneath the surface of the earth and recording any bulging on the surface. Volcanologists are often able to predict when a volcano is about to erupt. Often when there is a series of small earthquakes near a volcano they will be followed by a volcanic eruption.

Mount St. Helens, a famous volcano found in the state of Washington, had not erupted since the mid-1800s. In 1980, it erupted with a force said to be equal to ten million tons of dynamite! It was the most destructive eruption in the history of the United States. Many people lost their lives and hundreds of homes and entire forests were destroyed.

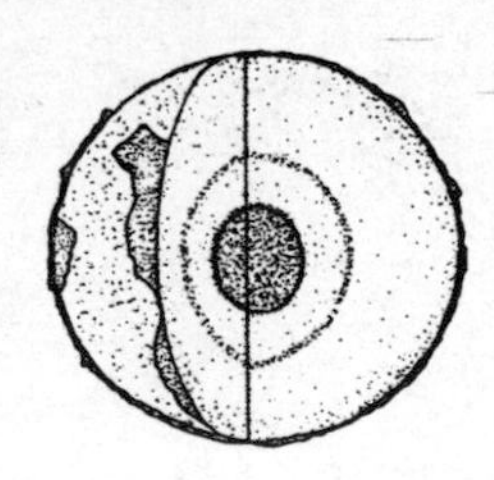

EARTH'S CRUST

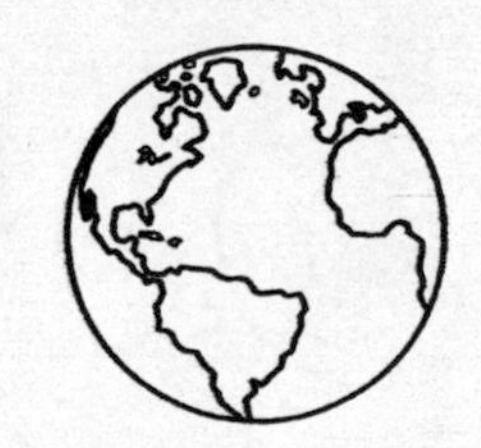

Volcanoes

Info Check

1. Write definitions for the following words:

   a) active volcano: ______________________________

   b) dormant volcano: ______________________________

   c) extinct volcano: ______________________________

2. Explain the term 'hot spot'. ______________________________

3. What is 'geothermal energy'? ______________________________

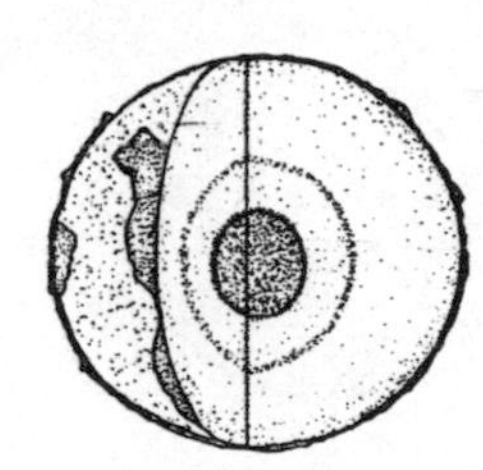

EARTH'S CRUST

4. Match each place in the first column with a geological event in the second column. You may have to do a little research!

a	Sicily		Paricutin
b	The Pacific Plate		hot spot
c	Washington		volcano belt
d	Iceland		geothermal energy
e	North Atlantic Ocean		hot spring
f	Hawaiian Islands		geyser
g	Yellowstone Park		Mt. Etna
h	Mexico		volcano belt
i	Mediterranean Sea		Surtsey
j	New Zealand		Mount St. Helens

5. Research one of the geological features from the chart above and write about it.

____
____
____
____
____
____
____
____
____
____

6. Explain the difference between 'lava' and 'magma'. ____________________

____
____
____

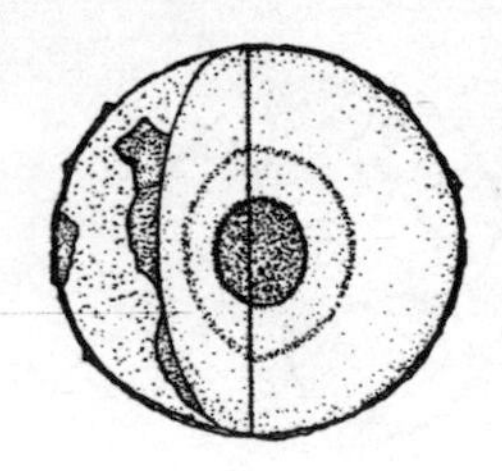

EARTH'S CRUST

Rocks and Minerals

Teacher Input

Overview

This component investigates the three main types of rock, and some of the properties by which rocks and minerals can be identified. Students will gain an understanding of the rock cycle as an ongoing process on the earth's crust.

Many additional activities can be added to this component if time allows. Rock collections can be displayed, and the students can participate in activities such as making crystals, using microscopes to view the crystal structures of rocks and minerals, performing streak, color and hardness tests, etc. A trip to a museum, or borrowing rocks and mineral kits available from museums would be worthwhile and interesting activities. Rocks lend themselves to many art activities such as rock painting and sand art. This would also a good time to explore clay.

The graphing activity in this component is only one of many that can be used to reinforce skills in mathematics using data collected about rocks and minerals.

Geography skills can be integrated by having students focus on mining in their province/ state or the world, using atlases, charts, films, etc. Check your school for kits entitled 'Mining Matters'. These kits are a great resource for rock samples and additional activities.

Resources

McConnell, Anita. The World Beneath Us. Facts on File Inc.; New York, ©1985.

Farndon, John. How the Earth Works. Reader's Digest Assoc.; New York, ©1992.

Markle, Sandra. Digging Deeper: Investigations into Rocks, Shocks and Other Earthly Matters. Lothrop, Lee and Shepard Books; New York, ©1987.

Curtis, Neil. Rocks and Minerals. Oxford University Press; New York, ©1998.

Symes, Dr. R. F. Eyewitness Book of Rocks and Minerals. Stoddart Publishing Company Limited; Toronto, Canada, ©1991.

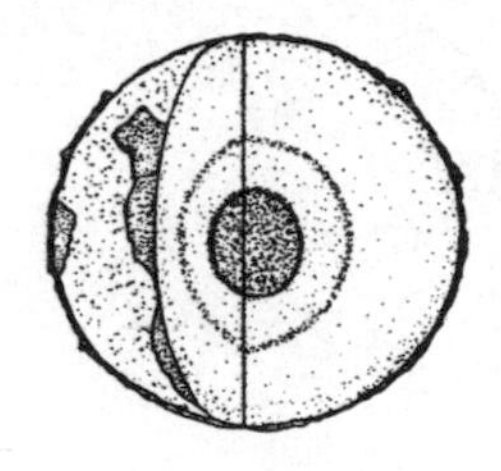

EARTH'S CRUST

Rocks and Minerals

Answers

<u>Info Check</u>: *(page 62)*

A few Examples:

1. **a)** Igneous rock is changed to sedimentary rock when igneous rock is worn into tiny bits of sand or sediment by weathering or erosion. The sediments are deposited in streams, or river beds where they eventually turn into sedimentary rock.
   b) Sedimentary rock is changed to metamorphic rock when it is subducted beneath the earth and changed by heat and pressure.
   c) Metamorphic rock that is subducted or heated in any way can be turned to magma, which can then find its way to the surface of the earth through volcanoes.
2. **a)** crystals, minerals **b)** twenty **c)** carbon **d)** inorganic
   e) cannot **f)** fossils **g)** oxygen and silicon
   h) igneous **i)** shale **j)** basalt **k)** marble
   l) magma **m)** all layers **n)** gold **o)** sedimentary
3.

Mineral	Color	Luster	Scale	Hardness
quartz	white	glassy	7	will scratch glass
calcite	white	glassy	3	can be scratched with a penny
feldspar	white	glassy	6	will scratch knife blade
gypsum	whites	pearly	2	can be scratched will fingernail
diamond	colorless	glassy	10	will scratch everything

4. Graphs will vary depending on scale used. Vertical scale should read, "THE PERCENTAGE OF ELEMENTS FOUND IN EARTH'S CRUST". Title should read, "ELEMENTS FOUND IN THE EARTH'S CRUST".

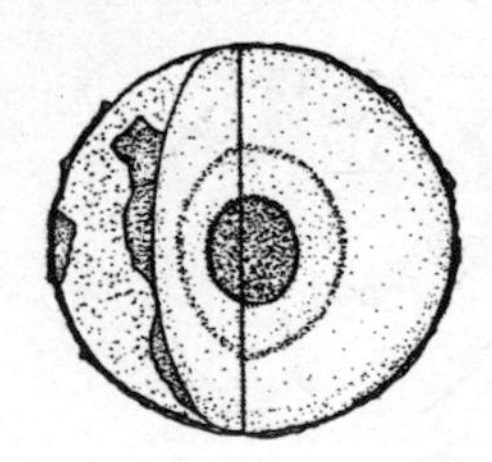

EARTH'S CRUST

Rocks and Minerals

Information Card #7

If you dig anywhere in the earth's crust, you'll eventually hit rock! An important part of geology is the study of rocks and minerals. Rocks are one of the most abundant materials found on our planet, making up the crust, mantle and core of the earth. Rocks come in a variety of shapes, colors and textures, and hold important clues to our planet's history.

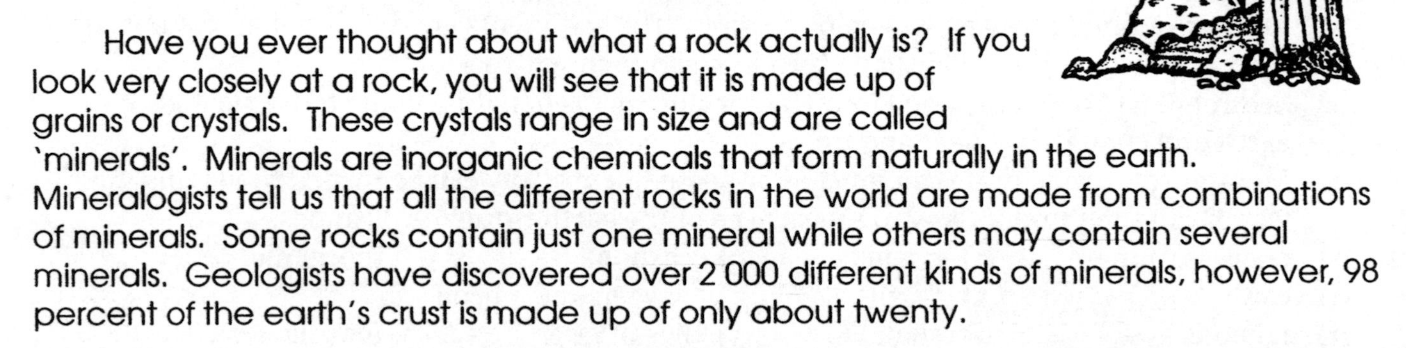

Have you ever thought about what a rock actually is? If you look very closely at a rock, you will see that it is made up of grains or crystals. These crystals range in size and are called 'minerals'. Minerals are inorganic chemicals that form naturally in the earth. Mineralogists tell us that all the different rocks in the world are made from combinations of minerals. Some rocks contain just one mineral while others may contain several minerals. Geologists have discovered over 2 000 different kinds of minerals, however, 98 percent of the earth's crust is made up of only about twenty.

All minerals have a certain chemical make-up, that is, they are made up of 'elements'. An element is a substance that cannot be broken down into a simpler substance. While some minerals, like gold, copper, sulphur, aluminum and magnesium are made up of just one element, most minerals consist of two or more elements. A diamond consists only of carbon. The atoms that make up the elements of a mineral bond together in very specific and orderly arrangements. This arrangement is what gives minerals their crystal shape. The shape of a crystal depends on the type of mineral. Quartz, for instance, forms long six-sided crystals and hatite, a form of salt, forms cubic shaped crystals.

The elements of silicon and oxygen account for more than 75 percent of the earth's crust. These two elements join together to form 'silicates' which are the most common of all mineral groups and make up 98 percent of all the rocks in the earth's crust. Two examples of silicates are sand and quartz.

The earth's crust consists of thousands of different types of rocks but each one belongs to one of three large groups depending on how it was formed. Geologists have named these three main groups 'igneous', 'sedimentary', and 'metamorphic' rocks.

The name 'igneous' comes from the Latin word 'ignis' which means 'produced by fire'. Igneous rock is formed when rock melts under great temperatures and then solidifies again. Igneous rock is formed in two ways. Granite, a coarse grained type of igneous rock, is formed when magma, that is being pushed up toward the crust, cools and hardens before it reaches the top. Granite is made of three main materials: quartz, mica and feldspar.

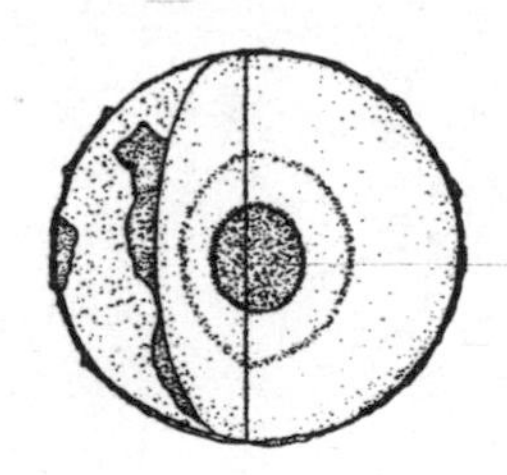

EARTH'S CRUST

Sedimentary rocks are layered rocks and are made from particles of 'sediment'. Sediment consists of bits of sand, soil, mud and small pebbles which have been worn off larger rocks by wind, water and ice. As sediment collects and settles down in lakes, rivers and oceans, it piles up in layers. As the layers build, the pressure created as more and more layers are added causes the sediment to pack together or solidify. Over thousands of years the sediments solidify and turn into sedimentary rock. Some sedimentary rock, like coal, chalk and limestone are formed from organic material such as shells, skeletons and other parts of plants and animals that once lived on the earth.

Sometimes, sedimentary rocks that are buried under enormous piles of sediment are buried deep by upheavals on the earth like earthquakes and volcanoes, are changed into metamorphic rock. The word 'metamorphic' comes from 'meta' which means 'change' and 'morphic' which means shape or form. Metamorphic rocks are rocks that have been changed by great temperatures or pressures in the earth's crust. They are usually harder and heavier than sedimentary rocks. Marble, slate and quartzite are all examples of metamorphic rocks. Slate was once shale, and marble was once limestone. The crust of the earth is always moving and changing. All three types of rock are constantly moving and changing from one type to another in what is called the "rock cycle". The changes, however, may take thousands and millions of years.

As igneous rock, for example, is worn down and carried away in water, it eventually becomes sedimentary rock. The sedimentary rock may be subjected to heat and pressure and turned into metamorphic rock, or it may be subducted beneath the surface of the earth during mountain building and melted to form magma. The magma hardens and turns into igneous rock and the cycle starts over. All rocks may have passed through the rock cycle many times over the billions of years since the earth was formed.

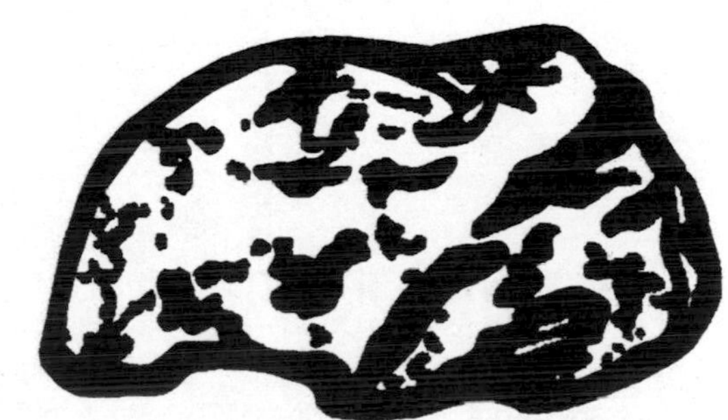

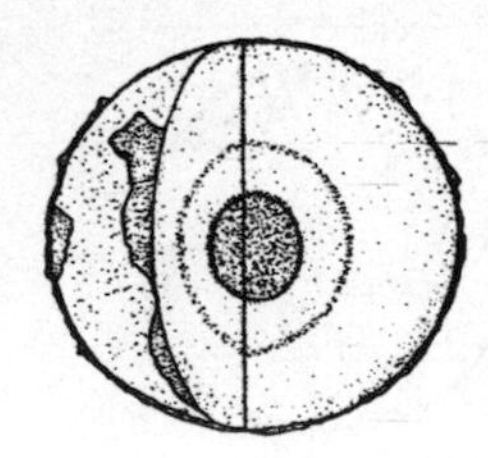

EARTH'S CRUST

Rocks and Minerals

Info Check

1. Explain, in the boxes, the geological processes at work as one type of rock is changed to another.

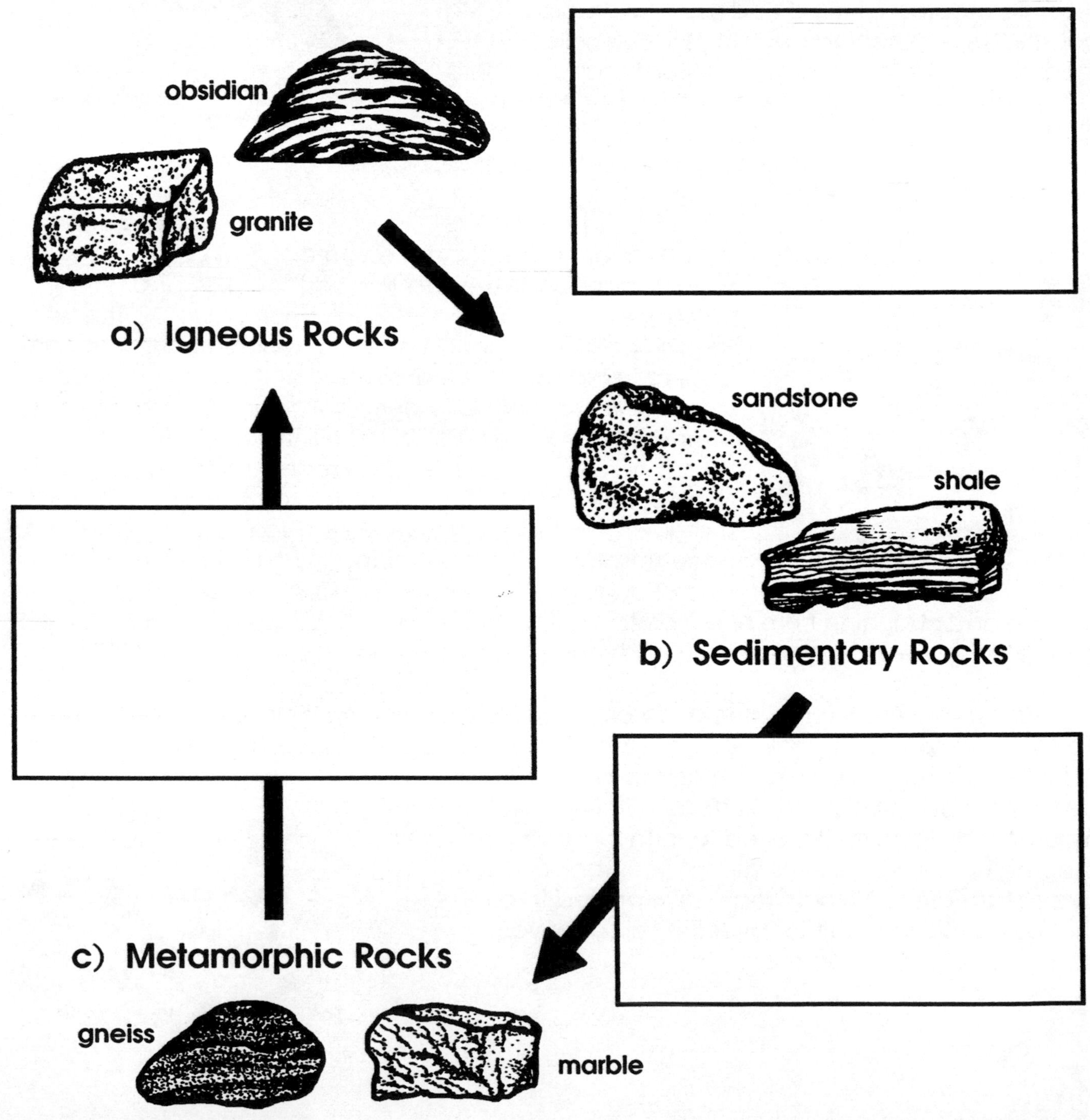

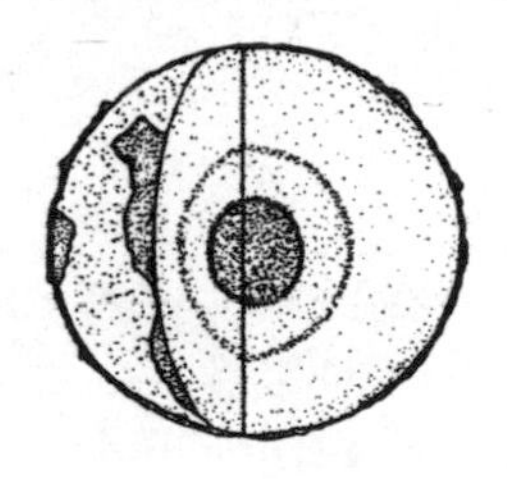

EARTH'S CRUST

2. Choose the correct word from those in the brackets to fill each space.

a) All rocks are composed of (**minerals, crystals**) ________________ called (**oxides, minerals**) ________________.

b) About 98 percent of the earth's crust is made up of about (**twenty, two thousand**) ________________ minerals.

c) A diamond is composed of (**carbon, sulphur**) ________________.

d) Minerals are (**inorganic, organic**) ________________ chemicals.

e) An element (**can, cannot**) __________ be broken down into simpler substances.

f) Sedimentary rock most often contains (**fossils, precious stones**) ______________.

g) More than 75 percent of the earth's surface consists of (**oxygen and hydrogen, oxygen and silicon, silicon and hydrogen**) ________________ and ________________.

h) The name (**igneous, metamorphic, sedimentary**) means 'formed from fire'. ________________

i) An example of sedimentary rock is (**slate, shale**) ________________.

j) An example of an igneous rock is (**sandstone, shale, basalt**) ________________.

k) An example of metamorphic rock is (**marble, shale, coal**) ________________.

l) Molten rock inside the earth is called (**igneous, magma, lava**) ________________.

m) Rock makes up (**the crust, the core, all layers**) ________________ of the earth.

n) A mineral consisting of just one element is (**gold, granite**) ________________.

o) Looking at a rock with many layers, one might guess that it is probably (**igneous, metamorphic, sedimentary**) ________________ rock.

EARTH'S CRUST

3. Minerals can be identified by one of several characteristics such as color, cleavage, hardness and luster. Some of these characteristics can be found in the charts below. The color of some minerals is shown in Chart A. The hardness of a mineral can be determined by what will scratch the mineral. Some common minerals and their rating on a hardness scale are shown in Chart B. The luster or shine of certain minerals is also an identifying characteristic. The luster of some minerals is shown in Chart C. Using the three charts, complete the physical characteristic chart for the minerals in Chart D.

Chart A

Hardness	Mineral	Can be scratched with a
1	talc	fingernail
2	gypsum	fingernail
3	calcite	copper penny
4	fluorite	steel knife
5	apatite	knife with pressure
		Will scratch
6	feldspar	a knife blade
7	quartz	glass and all previous
8	topaz	quartz and all previous
9	corundum	all except diamond
10	diamond	everything

Chart B

Color	Mineral
colorless	halite, diamond
white	quartz, calcite, gypsum, feldspar
black	mica
pale purple	fluorite
grey red	hermatite

Chart C

Luster	Mineral
glassy	diamond, calcite, quartz, feldspar
dull	hermatite
pearly	mica, gypsum, talc

Chart D

Mineral	Color	Luster	Scale	Hardness
quartz			7	will scratch glass
calcite				
feldspar	white			
gypsum				
diamond				

EARTH'S CRUST

4. The following table shows the eight main elements and the percentage of each found in the earth's crust. These eight elements make up 99 percentof all rock. Use the data to construct a bar graph of these elements. Label and choose a scale for your graph.

Element	%	Element	%
magnesium	1.9	sodium	2.3
potassium	2.4	calcium	4.1
iron	4.8	aluminum	8.3
silicon	28.9	oxygen	46.5

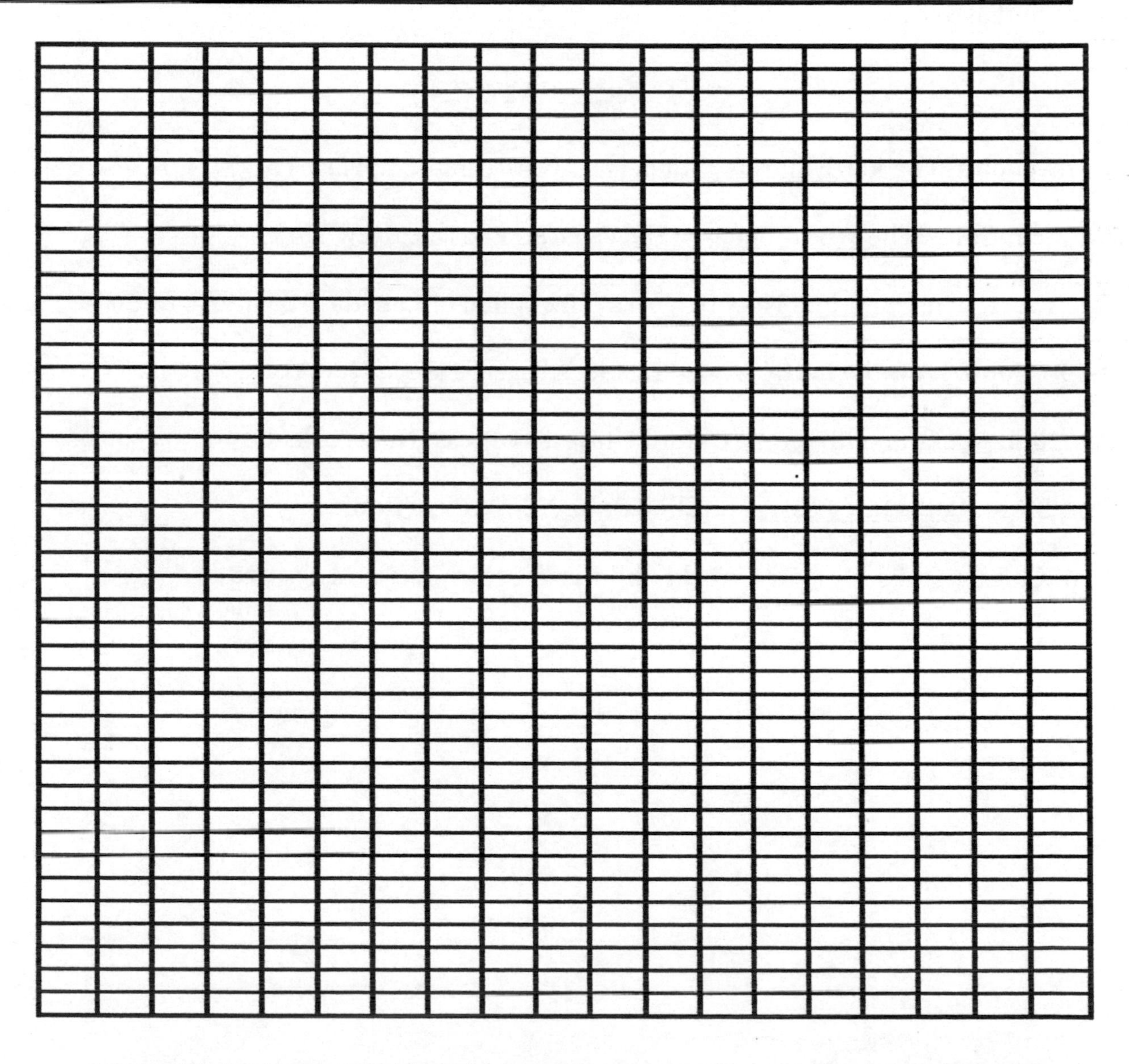

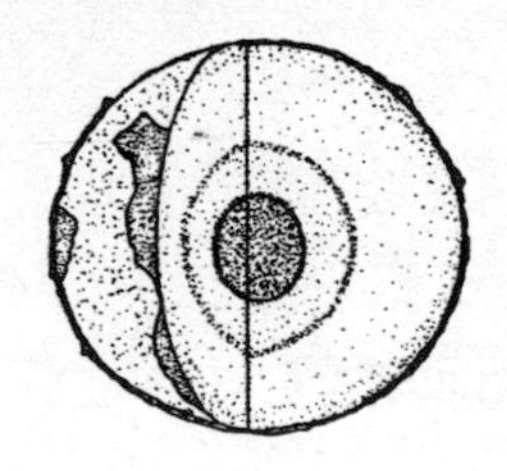

EARTH'S CRUST

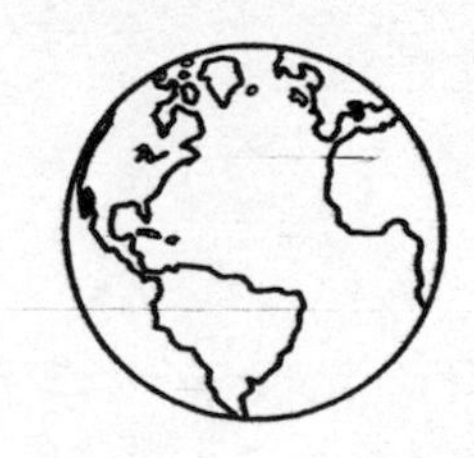

Fossils

Teacher Input

Overview

This component familiarizes the students with the importance of fossils to the science of geology. Students should have access to fossil specimens or several picture books. A visit to a museum to examine dinosaurs and other fossils would be most worthwhile. There are several good books on fossils available, and Pellant's book (see resources) is highly recommended for its pictures and activities.

Resources

Thackray, John. The Earth and Its Wonders. Larousse and Co.; New York, ©1980.

McConnell, Anita. The World Beneath Us. Facts on File Inc.; New York, ©1985.

Parker, Steve. The Earth and How It Works. MacMillan of Canada; Toronto, ©1989.

Farndon, John. How the Earth Works. Reader's Digest Assoc.; New York, ©1992.

Curtis, Neil. Rocks and Minerals. Oxford University Press; New York, ©1998.

Parker, Steve. Collecting Fossils. Sterling Pub.; New York, ©1997.

Pellant, Chris. Fossils. Dragon's World Children's Books; England, ©1994.

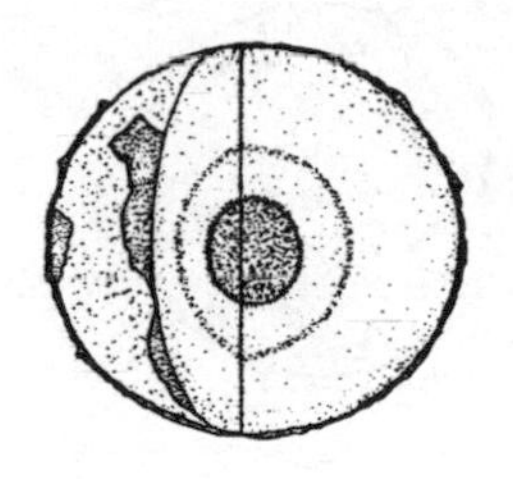

EARTH'S CRUST

Fossils

Answers

Info Check: ***(page 70)***

1. **a)** ***paleontologist*** – scientist who studies fossils
   b) ***petrified*** – wood or other organic material that has turned to stone
   c) ***geological column*** – a theoretical column cut through all the layers of rock since the beginning of the earth, would show a complete history of the earth
2. **a)** fossils are formed in different ways
   b) found in sedimentary rock
   c) formed from material such as teeth, bone, shell, bone, etc.
   d) most fossils come from sea plants and animals
3. See Fossils Information Card (p. 67, 2nd paragraph).
4. ***fossils*** – provide clues as to forms of life inhabiting the earth in earlier time periods – support the theory of continental drift, allows scientists to date rocks – provide clues to the climate and vegetation of earlier eras – provide information about the evolution of some species.
5. ***sedimentary***
6. ***mineralized fossil*** – formed when the plant or animal absorbs minerals and turns to stone mould fossil – formed when the remains rot away and form a hole
7. ***cast fossil*** – formed by making a mould and then filling the mould with a medium such as plaster (many examples in reference books – see Pellant's book)
8.

Pre-Cambrian	beginning of the earth until 600 million years ago
Paleozoic – sea plants and animals, reptiles	600 million to 225 million years ago
Mesozoic Era – dinosaurs	225 million to 65 million years ago
Cenozoic Era – mammals, humans	65 million until present

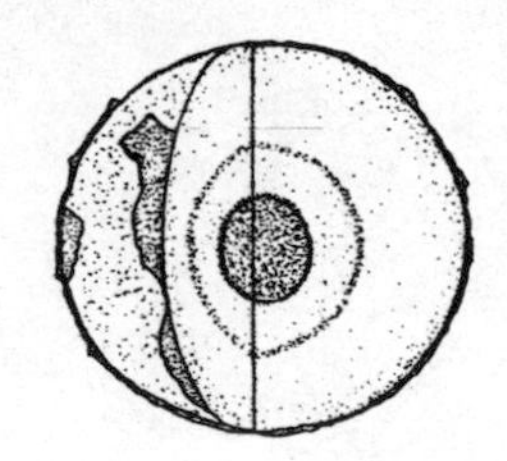

EARTH'S CRUST

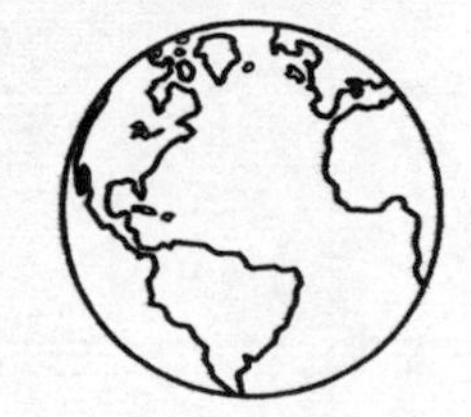

Fossils

Information Card #8

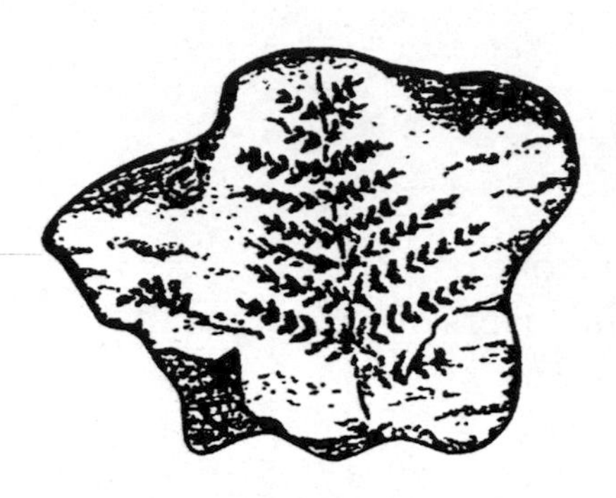

When most plants and animals die, they usually decay and are returned to the earth as soil. Sometimes, however the animal or plant is buried under the sand or at the bottom of a body of water, under thick layers of mud. In time, the plant or animal becomes a fossil. Fossils are the imprints or remains of organisms which lived on the earth in past geologic ages. The word 'fossil' comes from Latin and means 'something dug up'. Most fossils come from plants or animals that lived in or near water and had hard skeletons or shells. Rocks such as chalk and limestone are made almost entirely of tiny shell creatures. Even though many fossils are made from creatures that live near the sea, there are not many fish fossils. Can you think why?

Once the animal or plant is buried under the sand or mud, the fleshy parts soon rot away and only the hard parts of the animal or plant, like teeth, shells, wood stems, or bone is left. The hard parts are continually covered by layer after layer of sediment. Over hundreds of thousands of years, the layers of sediment under the immense pressure of each other turn to sedimentary rock, trapping the remains of the plant or animal inside. That is the reason why almost all fossils are found in sedimentary rock.

There are different types of fossils depending on how they were formed. Mineralized or 'petrified' fossils are formed when the remains absorb minerals from the surrounding material, and gradually turn to stone. If the remains rot away and leave a hole, a 'mould' fossil is formed. If the hole becomes filled with other minerals, a 'cast fossil' is formed.

Scientists can tell a great deal about the history of the earth by studying fossils. Paleontologists, scientists who study fossils, are able to identify organisms that have lived on the earth and may now be extinct, as well as a great deal of other information such as what the climate and landscape may have been like at the time. Today, scientists have a complete set of fossils showing the evolution of the horse from a very small forest living creature to a larger animal suited to life on the plains.

Fossils provide clues to support the idea that the earth's crust consists of several large floating plates that broke away from one super continent. For instance, plant fossils of identical and now extinct plants were found on both Brazil

EARTH'S CRUST

and Africa, reinforcing the idea that the two land masses may once have been joined. By studying which kind of fossil is found in a particular kind of rock, paleontologists can figure out when rock was formed. This enables scientists to put together an overall picture of what the earth was like at different times in the earth's history. This picture of the different geological periods in the history of the earth is called the 'fossil record'.

Scientists divide earth's history into geologic time periods: the Precambrian, Paleozoic, Mesozoic and Cenozoic Eras. Geologists refer to what is called the 'geological column' when talking about the history of rocks. Theoretically, if a column could be cut straight up and down through all the layers of sedimentary rock that have ever built up on the earth, the column would reveal a complete history of the earth. Each layer of rock would be labeled as a division of geological history. The large eras would be divided into smaller 'periods' of time. Of course, with all the shifting of the earth's surface, it is impossible to find an area like this on the earth.

The Archeozoic Era, which began with formation of the earth about 4.6 billion years ago, and the Proterozoic Era, which began about 1.6 million years ago, are often considered together as the Precambrain Era. Scientists have not found any fossils which show evidence of any life on land during this time. The rocks of the Precambrian Era indicate a great deal of volcanic activity on the earth at that time.

The next era, the Paleozoic Era, is also known as the Age of Ancient Life. It began 600 million years ago and lasted 375 million years. Fossils from this era are of sea plants and animals, and they show the first reptiles, insects, spiders, amphibians and land plants. Trees and plants, which grew in the swamps during this time, later turned to coal. The Appalachian Mountains were formed in the Paleozoic Era and there were many volcanic eruptions. The glaciers which covered great masses of land slowly melted.

Dinosaurs lived and then became extinct during the Mesozoic Era. The Mesozoic Era, the Age of Dinosaurs, began about 225 million years ago and ended about 155 million years later. It was at this time that the Rocky Mountains were created. Rocks containing fossils of the first dinosaurs are only found in rocks that are dated to be about 230 to 65 million years old. Rocks from about 65 million years ago start to show the remains of mammals.

The Cenozoic Era, which began 70 million years ago and continues today, is known as the Era of Mammals. The earth went through many changes during this era. The Himalayas and the Alps were formed, and there was a great change in the climate of the earth as it entered into an ice age. Glaciers covered a great deal of the land, and changed the face of the earth by creating lakes and rivers and depositing large amounts of rock.

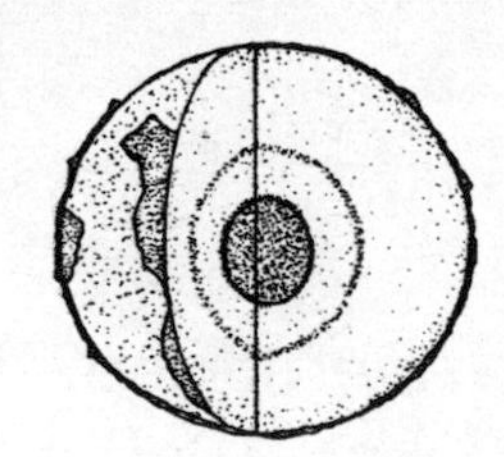

EARTH'S CRUST

Fossils

Info Check

1. Write definitions for the following words.

a) paleontologist: ______________________________

____

____

b) petrified: ______________________________

____

____

c) geological column: ______________________________

____

____

2. Write four facts about fossils:

a) ______________________________

b) ______________________________

c) ______________________________

d) ______________________________

3. Do some research to find a picture of a fossil of a trilobite. Draw it below.

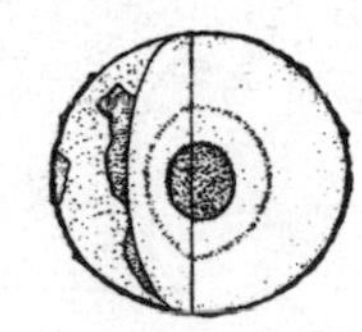

EARTH'S CRUST

4. Write three facts that show how information gained from fossils is important to our scientific knowledge of the earth.

a) ______________________________

____

____

b) ______________________________

____

____

c) ______________________________

____

____

5. In what type of rock would you look for fossils? ______________________________

6. Briefly describe how each of the following types of fossils are made.

a) mineralized fossil: ______________________________

____

____

b) mould fossil: ______________________________

____

____

7. Describe how you would make a cast fossil.

____

____

____

____

____

____

____

____

____

____

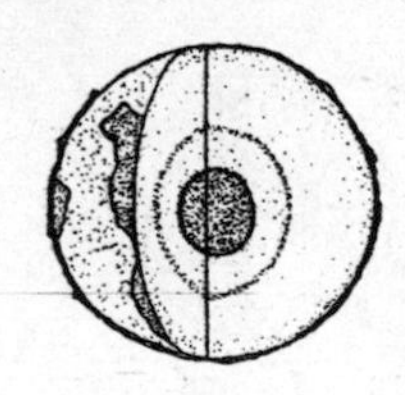

EARTH'S CRUST

8. Using information from Information Card "Fossils" and other resource materials, fill in the following chart. Show how many millions of years each era lasted, and draw labeled pictures of some of the different types of plants and animals that existed during each era.

The Geological Eras of the Earth

Name of Geologic Period	Millions of Years Ago
Pre-Cambrian	
Paleozoic Era	
Meszoic Era	
Cenozoic Era	

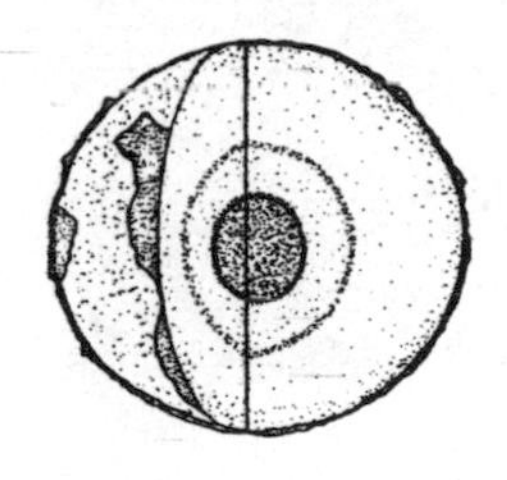

EARTH'S CRUST

Soil

Teacher Input

Overview

This component familiarizes the students with the composition and characteristics of soil. Students will learn about the effects of weathering and erosion on rocks as the first step in the soil-making process. If possible, students should participate in the collection and analysis of soil samples. Many simple experiments showing the process of erosion, as well as films on the topic are easy to find.

Resources

Allen, Dorothy Holmes. The Story of Soil. G.P. Putnam's Sons; New York, ©1976.

Bourgeois, Paulette. The Amazing Dirt Book. Kids Can Press; Toronto, ©1990.

Matthews, William H. Soils. F. Watts Publications; New York, ©1970.

McConnell, Anita. The World Beneath Us. Facts on File Inc.; New York, ©1985.

Parker, Steve. The Marshall Cavendish Science Project Book of the Earth. Marshall Cavendish Publications; New York, ©1986.

Bras, Judy. Geology: The Active Earth. National Wildlife Federation; Washington D.C., ©1988.

Farndon, John. How the Earth Works. Reader's Digest Assoc.; New York, ©1992.

Markle, Sandra. Digging Deeper. Lothrop, Lee and Shepard Books; New York, ©1987.

Pellant, Chris. Fossils. Dragon's World Children's Books; England, ©1994.

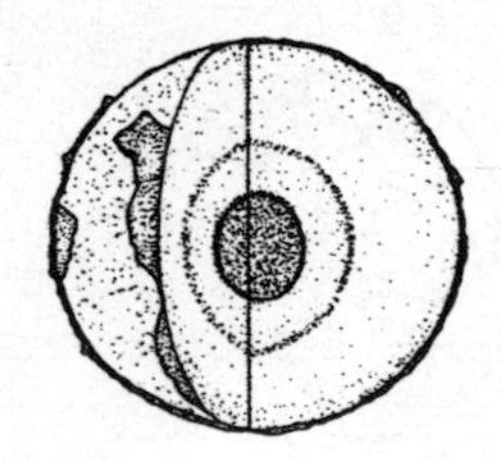

EARTH'S CRUST

Answers

Info Check: ***(page 77)***

1. **a)** climate
   b) living organisms
   c) topography of the land
   d) the type of rock which forms the soil (bedrock)
   e) time
2. **a)** bedrock
   b) biological weathering
   c) pedologist
   d) running water
   e) iron
   f) organic material
   g) humus
   h) loam
   i) chemical weathering

3. **a)** color
   b) texture
   c) porosity
   d) structure
   e) chemical composition
4. loam – soil with just the right amount of sand, clay, silt and humus
5. no – the clay in the soil is not porous and would not let water drain or sink through to the roots, would cause the soil to compact.
6. Answers may vary.

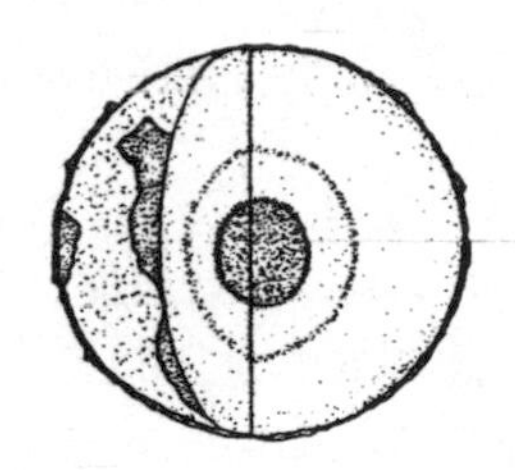

EARTH'S CRUST

Soil

Information Card #9

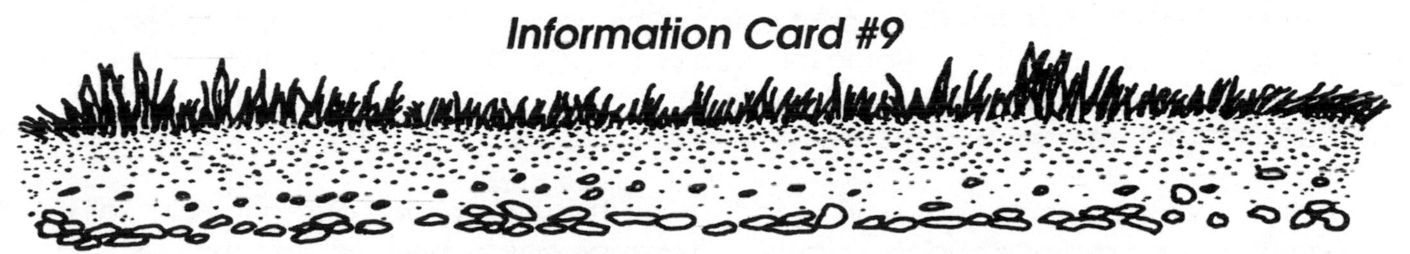

On top of the rocks that make up the earth's crust, the bedrock, there is a layer of soil. Without soil, there wouldn't be any life. Plants need soil in which to grow, and without plants most living things would not be able to exist. Soil, like air and water, is one of our most valuable resources.

Pedolgists are scientists who study soils. The name 'pedologist' comes from the Greek word 'pedon' which means 'soil'. Pedologists have found that many factors determine what type of soil will develop in a particular area. These factors are climate, living organisms, the topography of the land, the type of rock which forms the soil, and time. Generally, the formation of soil is a very slow process. It takes hundreds of years to make a layer of soil just centimeters deep. In some areas, soil may be millions of years old. Although all soils are not alike, they are all composed of inorganic minerals and organic material such as living organisms and the remains of dead plants and animals.

The soils of the earth vary greatly in thickness, color and composition depending on the area of the earth in which they are found. Each soil will be different depending on the type of bedrock it comes from. None of the rocks on the surface of the earth are permanent. Soil is formed when rocks are broken down through the processes of 'weathering' and 'erosion'. Weathering occurs when the earth's crust is broken down into fine pieces by the forces of nature such as wind, rain, snow, sun, and air. When weathered material is carried from one place to another, the process is known as erosion. Most erosion is caused by running water, however, moving ice and wind are also responsible for eroding the surface of the earth. Over many years, rivers and streams erode the landscape as they carry loose soil, sand and rock with them.

Temperature and rainfall have a great effect on the amount of weathering the rocks in an area undergo. In warm, moist climates, such as rainforests, rocks decompose quickly and soil is formed at a fairly fast rate. In hot, dry climates, like that of the desert, the weathering process is slower. In the temperate zones of the earth where there are great variations in climate, there are many weathering processes at work on rocks. Heat causes rocks to expand and crack while cold causes them to contract. Expansion and contraction cause the surface of the rocks to crumble. These changes are a result of 'mechanical weathering'. Sometimes soil finds its way into cracks made in the rock and plants begin to grow there. As plants spread their roots, the rock continues to crack and crumble. This process is known as 'biological weathering'.

EARTH'S CRUST

Rocks are also changed by 'chemical weathering', which is caused mostly by rain and stream water. As rain falls it absorbs carbon dioxide and other natural chemicals found in the air, and changes it to 'acid rain'. Often the air is polluted with other chemicals, which form different types of acids. When acid rain falls on rocks, it slowly eats away minerals in the rock. Some minerals are dissolved more quickly than others, and so the rate of soil formation may be quicker. Other factors such as erosion, and plant and animal life also determine how quickly soil will be formed in a particular area.

Plants and animals also have an important role in the formation and quality of soil in a given area. The remains of dead plants and animals decay and turn into 'humus', which enriches the soil and makes it better for growing plants. The plants living in the soil spread their roots down through the soil, allowing air and moisture to penetrate. As animals burrow, they excavate a great deal of material, which is brought to the surface. They make tunnels, which allow water to penetrate deep underground. Nesting materials such as leaves and twigs are carried deep underground where they decompose and add to the lower levels of soil. Worms, ants, and beetles tunnel through the soil breaking it up and allowing air and water to pass through. Animals also expose a great deal of rock to the atmosphere as they dig and burrow into the ground.

A pedologist examines several characteristics of a soil sample: texture, color, structure, chemical composition, and porosity. The texture of a soil depends on the size of the particles it contains, and may be graded according to the size of the majority of particles. The particles may be graded as coarse sand, find sand, silt, or clay. Most soils contain mixtures of sand, silt, and clay. Good soils contain approximately equal amounts of sand, silt, and clay. If a soil has too much sand it will allow too much water to sink away and thus plants will suffer from drought. Soils with too much clay pack together very tightly and don't allow roots to spread. When a soil is mixed with just the right amount of sand, clay, silt, and humus it is called 'loam' and is ideal for plants.

Just as important as the texture of a soil is its structure. The structure of a soil is determined by how the particles in the soil are clumped together. The texture and structure of the soil will determine its porosity, or the number of spaces it has. Soil that is to be used for growing plants needs to be porous enough to allow water and air to easily reach the roots of the plants.

The color of a soil gives an indication of the soil's history and the amount of air and organic material in the soil. Black and brown colors usually, but not always, indicate a good amount of organic material. If the soil is red there is a lot of iron present. Dark soils absorb more of the sun's heat and tend to be warmer.

The chemical composition of soil is important because plants get their nourishment from the soil. If the soil is deficient in elements such as oxygen, calcium, magnesium, sodium, potassium, and nitrogen, to name only a few, then the plants and every living thing that eats the plants will also be deficient in these nutrients.

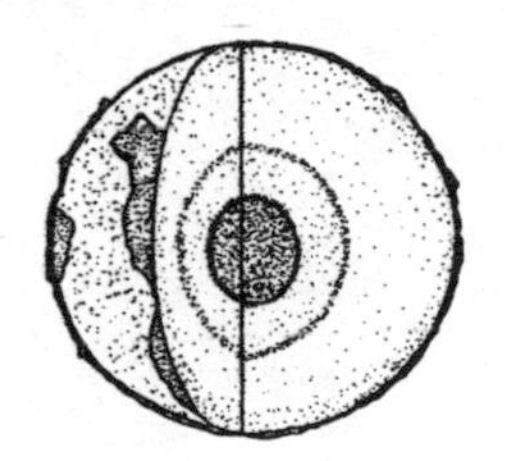

EARTH'S CRUST

Soil

Info Check

1. List the five factors that determine which type of soil will develop in a particular area.

   a) ______________________________
   b) ______________________________
   c) ______________________________
   d) ______________________________
   e) ______________________________

2. Fill in the blanks with words from the box.

bedrock	pedologist	loam	erosion	running water
humus	biological weathering	organic material	chemical weathering	

   a) Each soil will be different depending on the type of ______________ it comes from.

   b) Rock is broken down by the roots of plants in the process of ______________.

   c) A scientist who studies soils is called a ______________.

   d) Most erosion is caused by ______________.

   e) If soil is red, it indicates there is a lot of ______________ present.

   f) Decaying plant and animal material found in topsoil is called ______________.

   g) If a soil sample is black, it probably has a good amount of ______________.

   h) A soil with the right amounts of sand, silt, clay, and humus is called ______________.

   i) The effect of acid rain on rocks is called ______________.

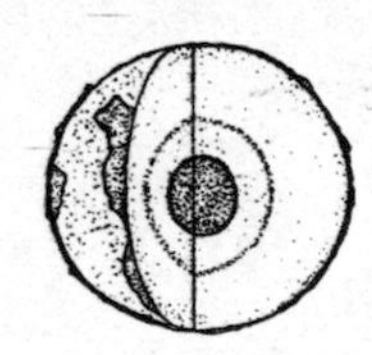

EARTH'S CRUST

3. The main characteristics of soil are:

a) ______________________________

b) ______________________________

c) ______________________________

d) ______________________________

e) ______________________________

4. What is loam? ______________________________

____

____

____

5. Would a soil which contains a lot of clay be considered a good soil by a farmer? Explain.______________________________

____

____

____

____

____

6. You are going to plant a garden. Explain how you will check the soil to assess whether it is suitable for growing vegetables.

____

____

____

____

____

____

____

____

____

____

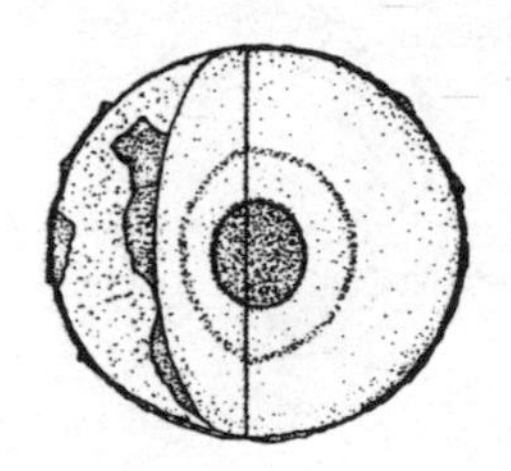

EARTH'S CRUST

Name: ______________________________ Date: ______________

Quiz #1

1. The study of the earth beneath us is known as the study of ______________.
2. The thinnest layer of the earth is the ______________.
3. Name the scientist known as 'the founder of modern geology'. ______________
4. The ancient Greek word 'geo' means ______________.
5. Most of the knowledge about the interior of the earth has come from studying ______________.
6. A paleontologist is a scientist who studies ______________.
7. Seismology is the study of ______________.
8. The Greek word for 'life' is ______________.
9. The lower part of the mantle is called the ______________.
10. The densest layer of the earth is the ______________.
11. Label the layers of the earth on the diagram below.

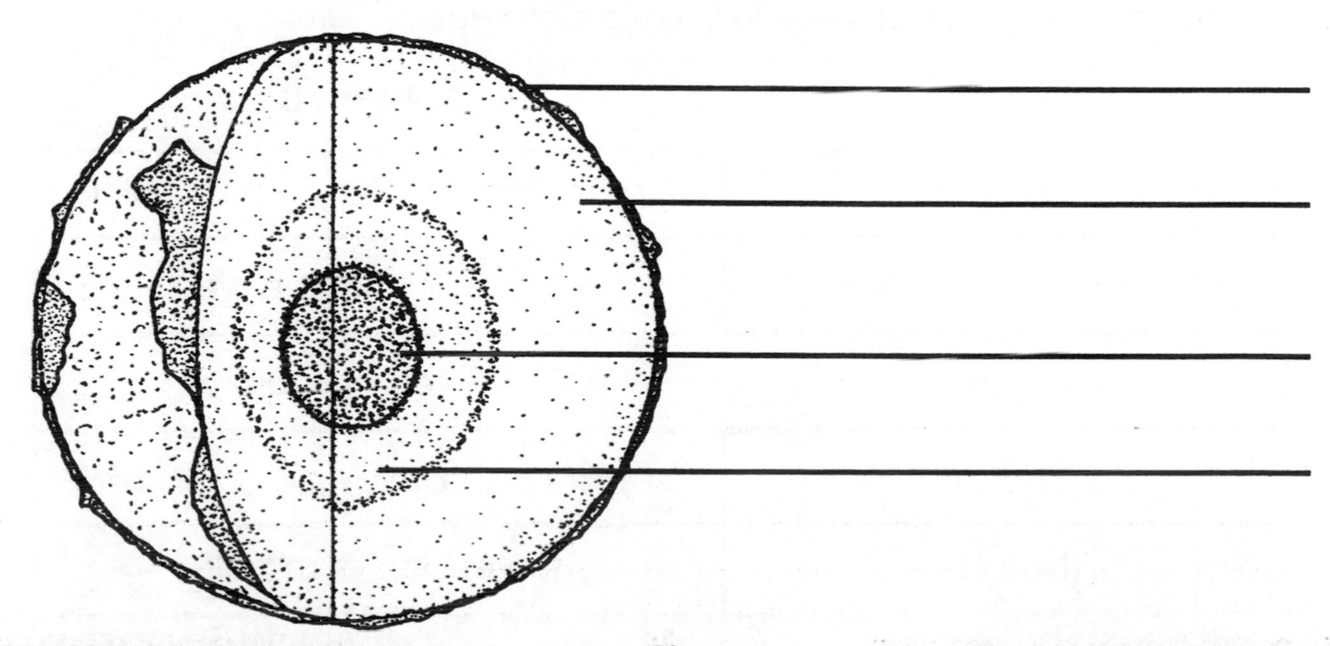

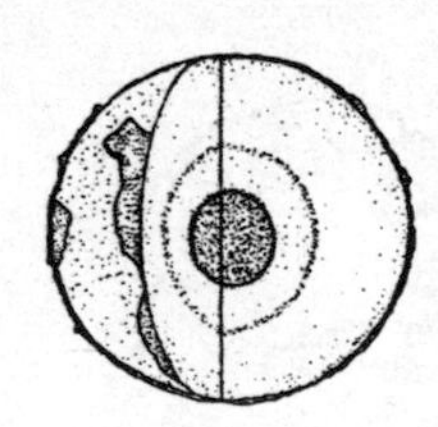

EARTH'S CRUST

12. Explain how scientists have learned what the inside of the earth is like.

13. Explain the meaning of the term 'lithosphere'.

14. Match each word in Column A with the best match from Column B.

	Column A		Column B
a)	molten		approximately 5 km - 40 km thick
b)	asthenosphere		layer beneath the crust
c)	crust		melted or liquid
d)	mantle		upper part of mantle and crust
e)	lithosphere		lower part of mantle

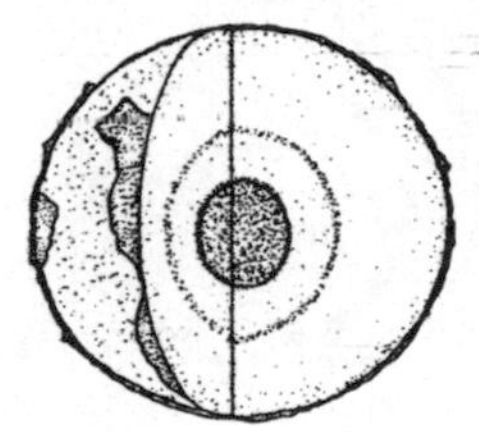

EARTH'S CRUST

Name: ____ Date: __________________

Quiz #2

1. The largest underwater mountain range is the __________________.
2. Scientists believe that the earth's crust consists of many __________________.
3. Six of the earth's tectonic plates carry all or part of a __________________.
4. It is believed that the continents once formed one super continent, which was called __________________.
5. The tectonic plates of the earth fit together like a giant __________________.
6. The highest mountains I the world are __________________.
7. The main types of mountains are fold mountains, dome mountains, block-fault mountains, and __________________ mountains.
8. When plates collide and the earth's crust forms 'waves' or 'wrinkles', ______________ mountains are formed.
9. When rock breaks, large cracks called __________________ are created.
10. In areas where tectonic plates are moving away from one another, molten rock called __________________ oozes up through the earth's crust.
11. The Atlantic Ocean is continually getting wider. Explain why this is happening.

____

____

____

____

____

____

____

____

____

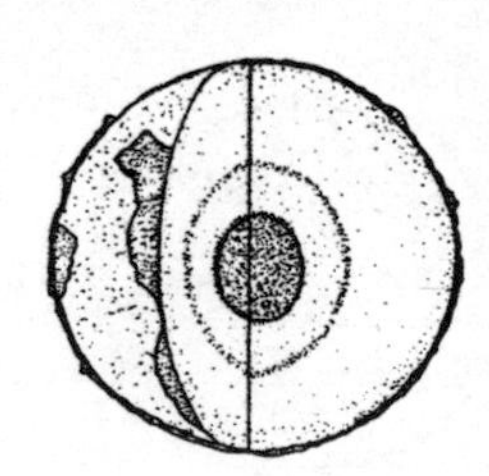

EARTH'S CRUST

12. Match each number on the map with the name of the tectonic plate in the chart below.

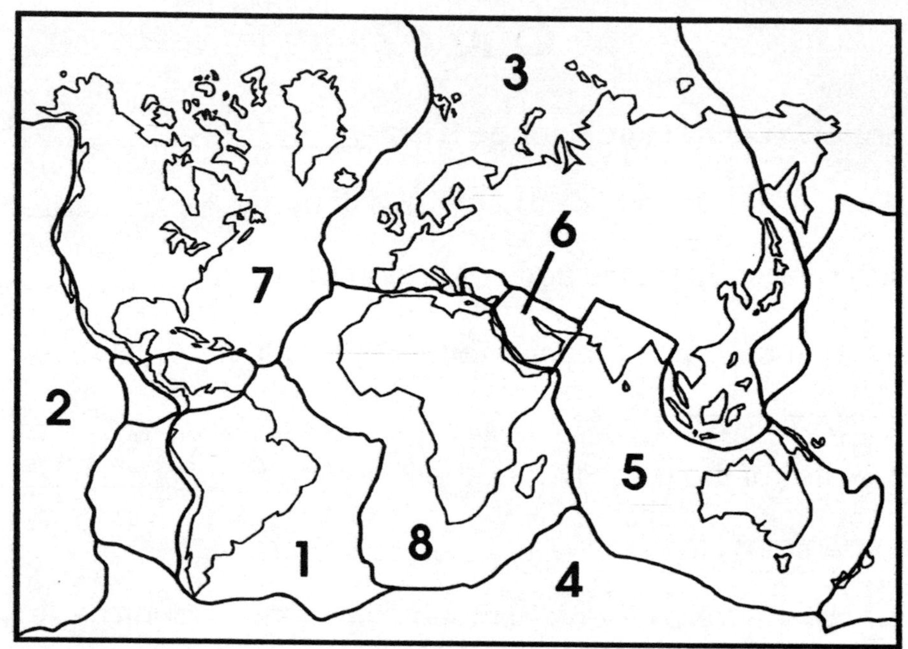

	North American Plate		Indo-Australian Plate
	African Plate		Eurasian Plate
	Pacific Plate		Arabian Plate
	South American Plate		Anarctic Plate

13. Explain the Continental Drift Theory.

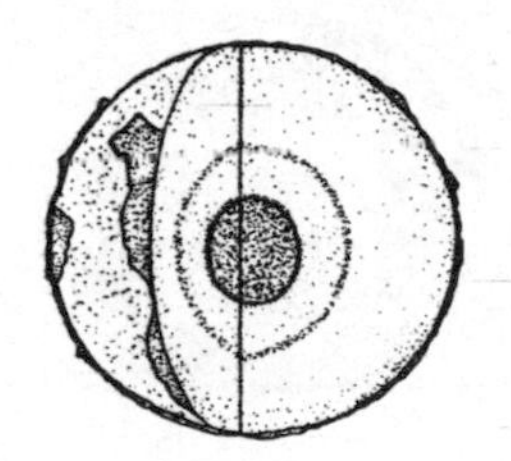

EARTH'S CRUST

Name: ____ Date: ____________________

Quiz #3

Write "**T**" beside each statement if it is true, or "**F**" if it is false.

1. ____ Earthquakes may take place anywhere on the earth.
2. ____ Most earthquakes take place along the fault lines.
3. ____ An extinct volcano is only 'sleeping'.
4. ____ The most active earthquake area is along the edges of the North American Plate.
5. ____ The San Andreas Fault is on the border of the Pacific Plate and the Nazca Plate.
6. ____ A famous volcano erupted in San Francisco in 1906.
7. ____ The Mercalli Scale measures the damage done during an earthquake.
8. ____ The focus of an earthquake is the place beneath the earth's surface that the seismic waves radiate from.
9. ____ Animals often give warning signs that volcanoes are about to erupt.
10. ____ The magnitude of an earthquake is a measure of how much damage it causes.
11. Briefly explain each of the following terms.

    a) seismic wave: ____

    ____

    ____

    b) epicenter: ____

    ____

    ____

    c) Ring of Fire: ____

    ____

    ____

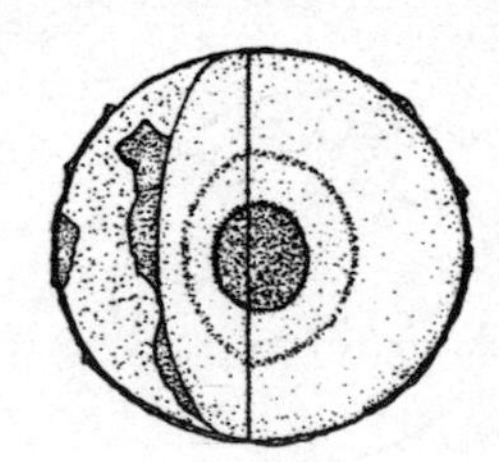

EARTH'S CRUST

12. Most of the volcanoes in the world are 'stratovolcanoes'. List two characteristics of a stratovolcano.

a) ____________________

b) ____________________

13. If you wanted to see a geyser, where would you go? ____________________

14. What is Surtsey? ____________________

____

____

____

____

____

____

15. a) What volcanic islands were formed from 'hot spots' beneath the surface of the earth? ____________________

b) What type of volcanoes formed these islands? ____________________

16. Match the famous volcanoes with their locations in the chart below.

a)	Mount St. Helens		Hawaii
b)	Surtsey		Mexico
c)	Mauna Loa		Washington
d)	Mt. Vesuvius		Italy
e)	Mt. Etna		Sicily
f)	Paricutin		North Atlantic Ocean

17. If you lived in Iceland, your house would probably be heated with ____________________ energy.

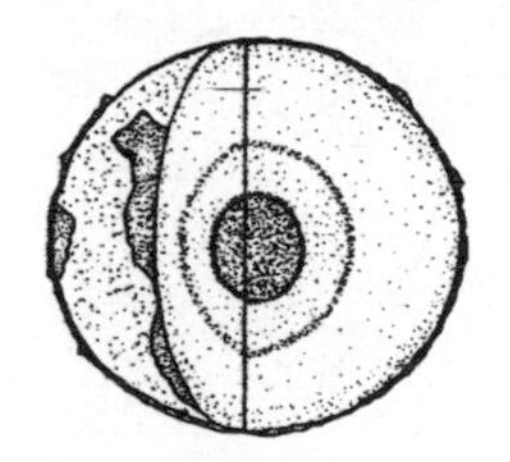

EARTH'S CRUST

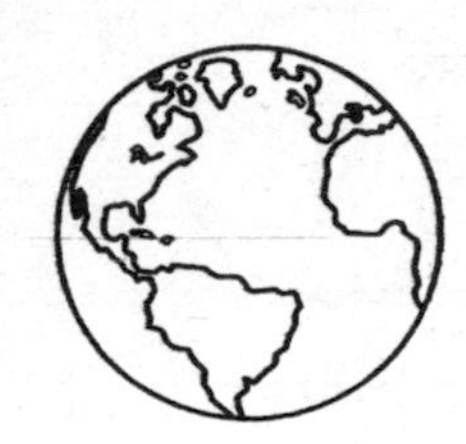

Name: ______________________________ Date: ____________

Quiz #4

1. Place each word or group of words in one space in the chart.

layered	granite
formed by fire	limestone
changed rock	marble

Igneous Rock	Metamorphic Rock	Sedimentary Rock

2. Explain what is meant by the 'rock cycle'. Draw a diagram to illustrate your answer.

____

____

____

____

____

____

____

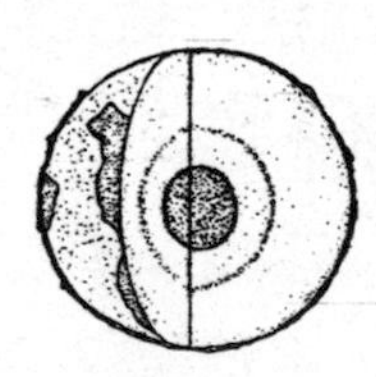

EARTH'S CRUST

3. Why are fossils important to our understanding of the earth?

____
____
____
____
____
____

4. In what type of rock would you look for fossils? ______________________

5. What type of plants and animals are usually found as fossils and why?

____
____
____

6. How have fossils supported the theory that the earth consists of huge tectonic plates?

____
____
____
____
____
____
____
____

7. Match the geological time periods with the forms of life appearing at that time.

	Geologic Time Period		Forms of Life Appearing at This Time
1	Paleozoic Era		first fish and reptiles
2	Mesozoic Era		woolly mammoth, early humans
3	Cenozoic Era		dinosaurs

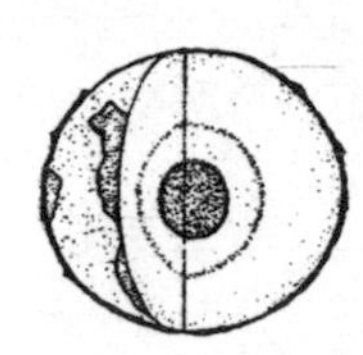

EARTH'S CRUST

8. You are trying to grow a plant for a science fair. You want it to be the healthiest plant ever. What type of soil will ensure that your plant has all the nutrients it needs? In the flowerpot, label the amounts of each material that will be in the soil you choose.

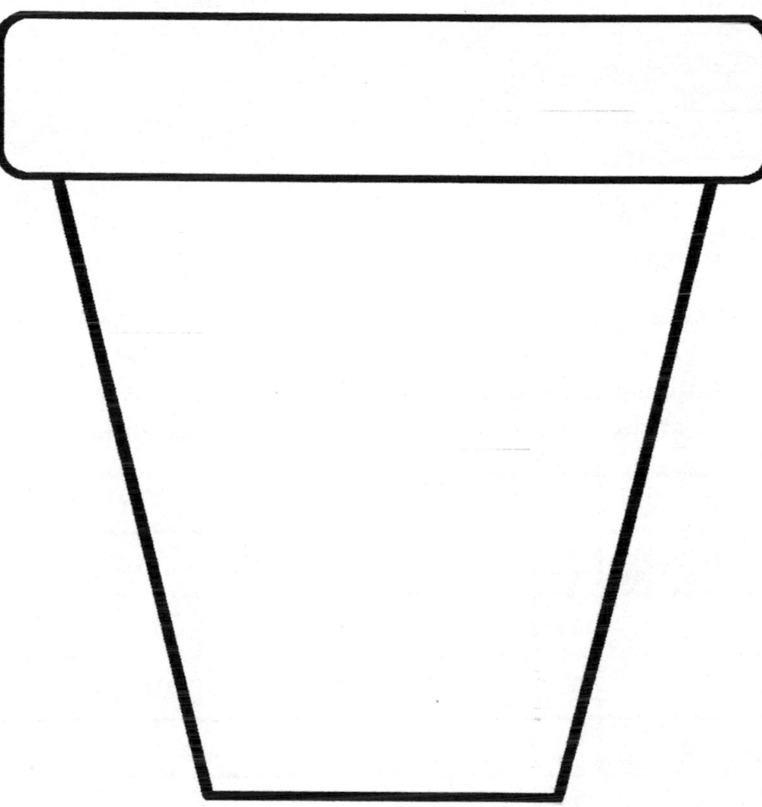

9. Explain the three types of weathering and give examples:

   a) chemical weathering: ______________________________
   ____
   ____
   ____

   b) mechanical weathering: ______________________________
   ____
   ____
   ____

   c) biological weathering: ______________________________
   ____
   ____
   ____

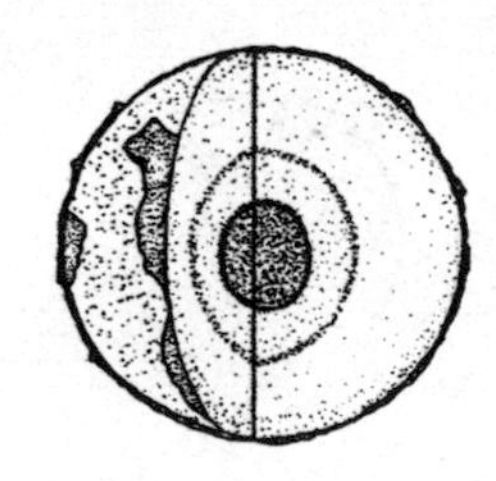

EARTH'S CRUST

Quiz #1 Answers (p. 79)

1. geology 2. crust 3. James Hutton 4. earth 5. earthquakes
6. fossils 7. earthquakes 8. bio 9. asthenosphere 10. inner core

11.

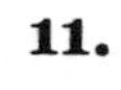

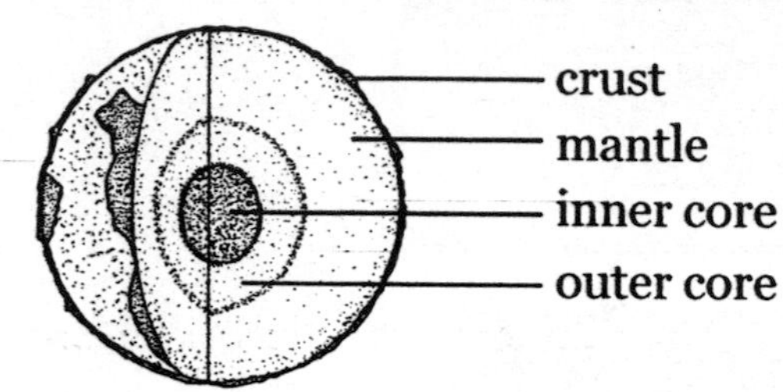

12. Scientists have learned about the inside of the earth by studying earthquakes. See page 21, paragraph 2.
13. The lithosphere is comprised of the crust and the rigid upper layer of the mantle. It is made up of tectonic plates that move on top of the lower mantle or asthenosphere.
14.

a)	molten	c)	approximately 5 km - 40 km thick
b)	asthenosphere	d)	layer beneath the crust
c)	crust	a)	melted or liquid
d)	mantle	e)	upper part of mantle and crust
e)	lithosphere	b)	lower part of mantle

Quiz #2 Answers (p. 81)

1. Mid-Atlantic Ridge 2. plates 3. continent 4. Pangaea 5. jigsaw puzzle
6. Himalayas 7. volcanic 8. fold 9. faults 10. magma
11. See answer on page 28, question #6.
12.

7	North American Plate	5	Indo-Australian Plate
8	African Plate	3	Eurasian Plate
2	Pacific Plate	6	Arabian Plate
1	South American Plate	4	Anarctic Plate

13. See answer on page 28, question #4.

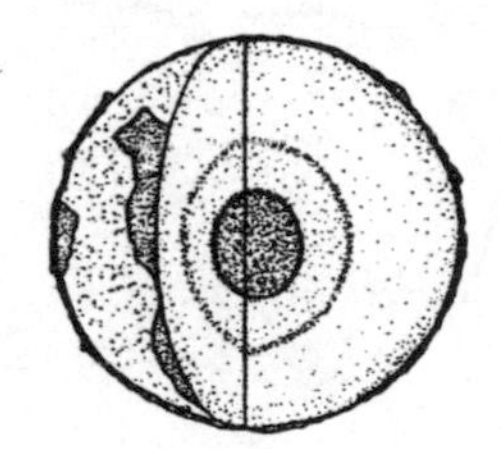

EARTH'S CRUST

Quiz #3 Answers (p. 83)

1. True
2. True
3. False
4. False – the Pacific Plate
5. False – the Pacific Plate and the North American Plate
6. False – it was an earthquake
7. True
8. True
9. False – they often give warning signs of earthquakes
10. False – it is a measure of the energy
11. a) ***Seismic wave*** – shock waves in the ground caused by earthquakes
    b) ***epicenter*** – the spot on the surface of the earth directly above the focus
    c) ***Ring of Fire*** – the area around the edges of the Pacific plate which is known for its many volcanoes and earthquake activity
12. ***stratovolcanoes*** – magma is hot and sticky, mixed with steam and gases
    a) caused by subduction of a plate
    b) spectacular eruptions
13. Yellowstone Park, New Zealand, Iceland
14. Surtsey is a volcanic island in the North Atlantic formed from an underwater volcanic eruption, near Iceland in 1963
15. a) Hawaiian Islands
    b) shield volcanoes
16.

1	Mount St. helens	3	Hawaii
2	Surtsey	6	Mexico
3	Mauna Log	1	Washington
4	Mt. Vesuvius	4	Italy
5	Mt. Etna	5	Sicily
6	Paricutin	2	North Atlantic Ocean

17. geothermal

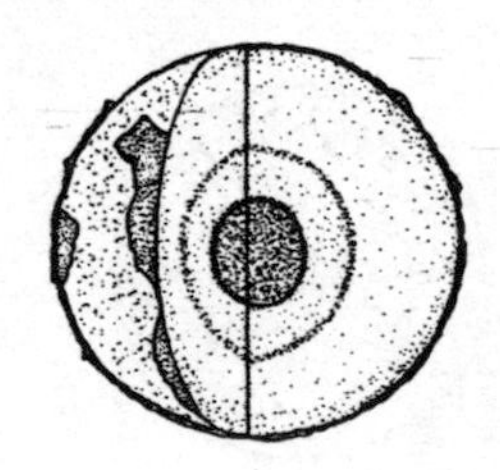

EARTH'S CRUST

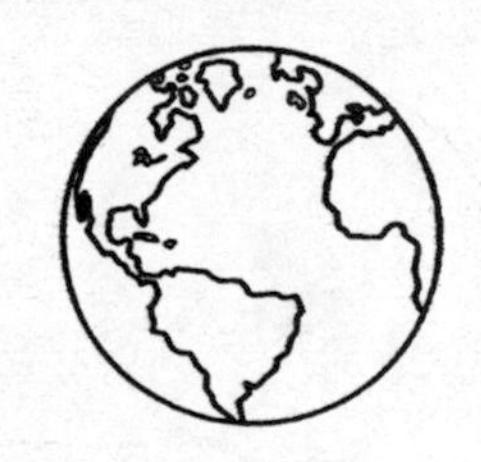

Quiz #4 Answers (p. 85)

1.

Ianeous Rock	Metamorphic Rock	Sedimentary Rock
formed by fire	changed rock	layered rock
aranite	marble	limestone

2. The Rock Cycle – see diagram Rocks and Minerals – Info Check p. 62
3. Fossils - provide evidence of past geological ages and the life forms that existed
   - help scientists to determine how forms of life living today have evolved over time
4. sedimentary
5. – sea plants and animals because of their shells and because much sedimentary rock formed from river beds
6. - fossils provide evidence to support the Continental Drift Theory, i.e. same fossils found on the continent of Africa and the continent of South America
   - plant fossils found in Brazil and Africa
7.

	Geologic Time Period		Forms of Life Apearing at this Time
1	Paleozoic Era	1	first fish and reptiles
2	Mesozoic Era	3	woolly mammoth, early humans
3	Cenozoic Era	2	dinosaurs

8. The pot should contain equal amounts of silt, sand, and clay. An above average answer would include the addition of humus.
9. **a)** chemical weathering – occurs on rock surfaces as a result of 'acid rain' and is a real problem in cities where there is a lot of pollution in the atmosphere. Buildings and monuments, etc. often suffer from chemical erosion. In areas where there is a lot of rainfall, rock dissolves quickly.
   b) mechanical weathering – is the erosion caused by running water, ice, or wind
   c) biological weathering – is erosion caused by living things.

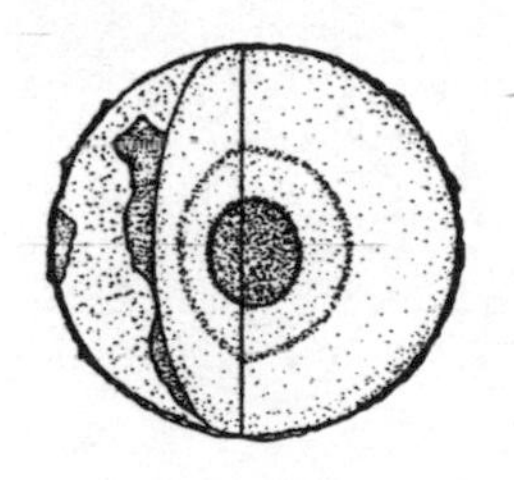

EARTH'S CRUST

Research Assignment

Research and prepare a presentation on one of the topics given. Your presentation will consist of three components:

a) A written report which adequately and clearly explains the topic.

b) Visual additions such as maps, diagrams, pictures, photographs, drawings, models, etc. which demonstrate the topic researched.

c) An oral presentation which will be assessed on organization and knowledge of the topic, clarity of voice, the material presented and the interest generated on the topic.

Points to Remember:

1. Your written work should be written neatly or typed on a computer.
2. Your diagrams, drawings and maps, etc., should be colored and labeled neatly, and be relevant to your topic.
3. Your written work must include a bibliography.
4. Your oral presentation will be ____ minutes in length.
5. ______________________________
6. ______________________________
7. ______________________________
8. ______________________________

Read the research topics and choose one that interests you. Before committing to a topic, it is a good idea to check the availability of resource material. You may wish to visit the library, etc., to make certain you will be able to find enough information on your topic.

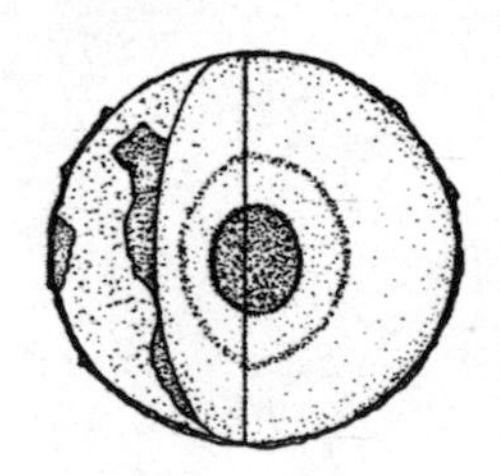

EARTH'S CRUST

Research Topics

1. For thousands of years ancient people from different cultures have tried to explain volcanic eruptions and earthquakes through myths and legends. Research and retell one of these ancient legends.

2. Scientists who study volcanoes are called 'volcanologists'. With great courage and specialized equipment, they observe the activity of volcanoes. Research the job of the volcanologist. In your presentation, include the types of technology volcanologists use and explain the importance of their work.

3. In March, 1980, Mount St. Helens erupted with what has been described as the force of ten million tons of dynamite. The eruption was the most destructive in the United States. Research Mount St. Helens.

4. Most books about volcanoes include the story about a farmer who had a volcano erupt in his field. The name of this famous volcano is Paricutin. Research Paricutin and retell the story of this famous volcano.

5. The ancient Roman city of Pompeii was buried under volcanic ash for 2 000 years. In 1748, it was dug up. Research Pompeii and write about what was found.

6. Iceland and the surrounding islands are volcanic islands. In 1963, a volcano near Iceland erupted and formed a new island. The name of this island is Surtsey. Research this new island, explaining its formation and the formation of the other islands, such as Iceland, that are in the same area.

7. There are different types of volcanoes. Research volcanoes in general, explaining in detail the characteristics of the different types.

8. The African and the Eurasian plates meet in an area of the Mediterranean Sea and have caused many earthquakes and volcanic eruptions. A famous volcano in this area is Mount Etna, which is Europe's most active volcano. Research Mount Etna, which last erupted in 1992.

9. In 1906, there was an earthquake in San Francisco that measured 8.25 on the Richter Scale. San Francisco is situated on the San Andreas Fault. Research this great earthquake and the earthquake zone in which is it located.

10. Seismology is the science of earthquakes. Research the study of earthquakes, include the job of the seismologist and the technology such as the seismograph and how it is used. Include information about the prediction of earthquakes, relief and rescue strategies, and steps taken to minimize damage from earthquakes.

EARTH'S CRUST

11. Research the science of paleontology and include information on the job of the paleontologist as well as information about fossils, example: how they are formed, different types, where found, importance of, etc.

12. Fossils provide a record of the earth's history that geologists have divided into geological time periods. Research the different time periods in the history of the earth.

13. The Mid-Atlantic Ridge is the longest mountain chain in the world. Research its formation and characteristics.

14. The minerals that we use for the thousands of products in our every day lives must be extracted from the earth's crust. Some minerals have to be mined. Research to find out about the different mining methods and the areas of the world where important mineral resources come from. Pay particular attention to any minerals that are mined in your country, and how their extraction affects the environment.

15. Oil is a fossil fuel. Research to find out how this resource is formed, its uses, and how it is obtained from the earth.

16. Research mountains, the different types, and how they are formed. Include information about the large mountain ranges of the world, their formation and type, and their effect on the area where they are located (example: climate, wildlife, population, etc.).

17. Many scientists are famous for their contribution to the earth sciences. Research one or more of the following people and report on their contribution to our knowledge of the earth: Alfred Wegener, James Hutton, Alexander von Humboldt, Charles Lyall, Charles F. Richter, Grove Karl Gilbert, William Smith. You may add other earth scientists to this list.

18. ____

____

____

____

19. ____

____

____

____

20. ____

____

____

____

EARTH'S CRUST

EARTH'S CRUST

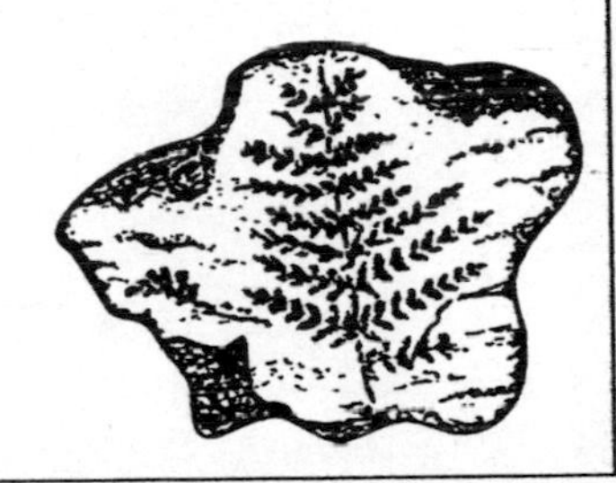

EARTH'S CRUST

EARTH'S CRUST

EARTH'S CRUST

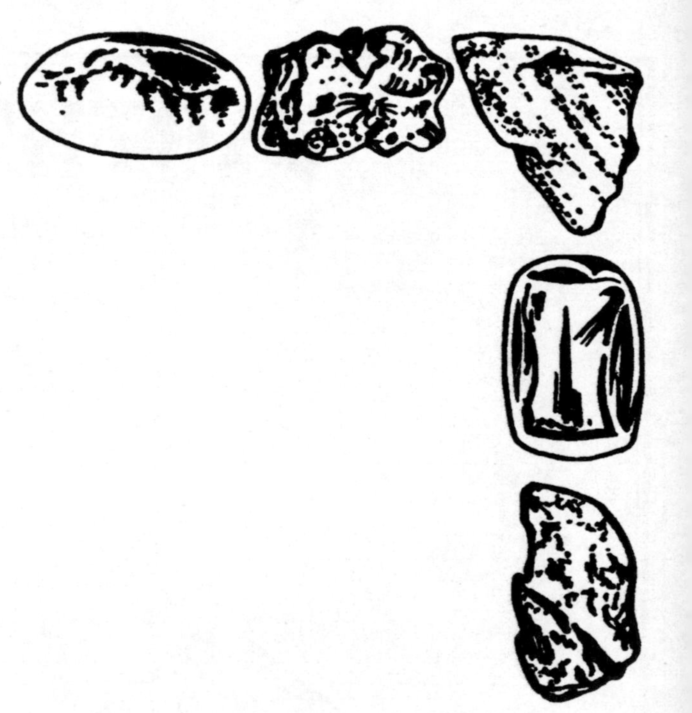

Publication Listing

Code #	Title and Grade
SSC1-12	A Time of Plenty Gr. 2
SSN1-92	Abel's Island NS Gr. 4-6
SSF1-16	Aboriginal Peoples of Canada Gr. 7-8
SSK1-31	Addition & Subtraction Drills Gr. 1-3
SSK1-28	Addition Drills Gr. 1-3
SSY1-04	Addition Gr. 1-3
SSN1-174	Adv. of Huckle Berry Finn NS Gr. 7-8
SSB1-63	African Animals Gr 4-6
SSB1-29	All About Bears Gr. 1-2
SSF1-08	All About Boats Gr. 2-3
SSJ1-02	All About Canada Gr. 2
SSB1-54	All About Cattle Gr. 4-6
SSN1-10	All About Colours Gr. P-1
SSB1-93	All About Dinosaurs Gr. 2
SSN1-14	All About Dragons Gr. 3-5
SSB1-07	All About Elephants Gr. 3-4
SSB1-68	All About Fish Gr. 4-6
SSN1-39	All About Giants Gr. 2-3
SSH1-15	All About Jobs Gr. 1-3
SSH1-05	All About Me Gr. 1
SSA1-02	All About Mexico Gr. 4-6
SSR1-28	All About Nouns Gr. 5-7
SSF1-09	All About Planes Gr. 2-3
SSB1-33	All About Plants Gr. 2-3
SSR1-29	All About Pronouns Gr. 5-7
SSB1-12	All About Rabbits Gr. 2-3
SSB1-58	All About Spiders Gr. 4-6
SSA1-03	All About the Desert Gr. 4-6
SSA1-04	All About the Ocean Gr. 5-7
SSZ1-01	All About the Olympics Gr. 2-4
SSB1-49	All About the Sea Gr. 4-6
SSK1-06	All About Time Gr. 4-6
SSF1-07	All About Trains Gr. 2-3
SSH1-18	All About Transportation Gr. 2
SSB1-01	All About Trees Gr. 4-6
SSB1-61	All About Weather Gr. 7-8
SSB1-06	All About Whales Gr. 3-4
SSPC-26	All Kinds of Clocks B/W Pictures
SSB1-110	All Kinds of Structures Gr. 1
SSH1-19	All Kinds of Vehicles Gr. 3
SSF1-01	Amazing Aztecs Gr. 4-6
SSB1-92	Amazing Earthworms Gr. 2-3
SSJ1-50	Amazing Facts in Cdn History Gr. 4-6
SSB1-32	Amazing Insects Gr. 4-6
SSN1-132	Amelia Bedelia–Camping NS 1-3
SSN1-68	Amelia Bedelia NS 1-3
SSN1-155	Amelia Bedelia-Surprise Shower NS 1-3
SSA1-13	America The Beautiful Gr. 4-6
SSN1-57	Amish Adventure NS 7-8
SSF1-02	Ancient China Gr. 4-6
SSF1-18	Ancient Egypt Gr. 4-6
SSF1-21	Ancient Greece Gr. 4-6
SSF1-19	Ancient Rome Gr. 4-6
SSQ1-06	Animal Town – Big Book Pkg 1-3
SSQ1-02	Animals Prepare Winter – Big Book Pkg 1-3
SSN1-150	Animorphs the Invasion NS 4-6
SSN1-53	Anne of Green Gables NS 7-8
SSB1-40	Apple Celebration Gr. 4-6
SSB1-04	Apple Mania Gr. 2-3
SSB1-38	Apples are the Greatest Gr. P-K
SSB1-59	Arctic Animals Gr. 4-6
SSN1-162	Arnold Lobel Author Study Gr. 2-3
SSPC-22	Australia B/W Pictures
SSA1-05	Australia Gr. 5-8
SSM1-03	Autumn in the Woodlot Gr. 2-3
SSM1-08	Autumn Wonders Gr. 1
SSN1-41	Baby Sister for Frances NS 1-3
SSPC-19	Back to School B/W Pictures
SSC1-33	Back to School Gr. 2-3
SSN1-224	Banner in the Sky NS 7-8
SSN1-36	Bargain for Frances NS 1-3
SSB1-82	Bats Gr. 4-6
SSN1-71	BB – Drug Free Zone NS Gr. 1-3
SSN1-88	BB – In the Freaky House NS 1-3
SSN1-78	BB – Media Madness NS 1-3
SSN1-69	BB – Wheelchair Commando NS 1-3
SSN1-119	Be a Perfect Person-3 Days NS 4-6
SSC1-15	Be My Valentine Gr. 1
SSD1-01	Be Safe Not Sorry Gr. P-1
SSN1-09	Bear Tales Gr. 2-4
SSB1-28	Bears Gr. 4-6
SSN1-202	Bears in Literature Gr. 1-3
SSN1-40	Beatrix Potter Gr. 2-4
SSN1-129	Beatrix Potter: Activity Biography Gr. 2-4
SSB1-47	Beautiful Bugs Gr. 1
SSB1-21	Beavers Gr. 3-5
SSN1-257	Because of Winn-Dixie NS Gr. 4-6
SSR1-53	Beginning Manuscript Gr. Pk-2
SSR1-54	Beginning Cursive Gr. 2-4
SSR1-57	Beginning and Practice Manuscript Gr. PK-2
SSR1-58	Beginning and Practice Cursive Gr. 2-4
SSN1-33	Bedtime for Frances NS 1-3
SSN1-114	Best Christmas Pageant Ever NS Gr. 4-6
SSN1-32	Best Friends for Frances NS Gr. 1-3
SSB1-39	Best Friends Pets Gr. P-K
SSN1-185	BFG NS Gr. 4-6
SSJ1-61	Big Book of Canadian Celebrations Gr. 1-3
SSJ1-62	Big Book of Canadian Celebrations Gr. 4-6
SSN1-35	Birthday for Frances NS Gr. 1-3
SSN1-107	Borrowers NS Gr. 4-6
SSC1-16	Bouquet of Valentines Gr. 2
SSN1-29	Bread & Jam for Frances NS Gr. 1-3
SSN1-63	Bridge to Terabithia NS Gr. 4-6
SSY1-24	BTS Numeración Gr. 1-3
SSY1-25	BTS Adición Gr. 1-3
SSY1-26	BTS Sustracción Gr. 1-3
SSY1-27	BTS Fonética Gr. 1-3
SSY1-28	BTS Leer para Entender Gr. 1-3
SSY1-29	BTS Uso de las Mayúsculas y Reglas de Puntuación Gr. 1-3
SSY1-30	BTS Composición de Oraciones Gr. 1-3
SSY1-31	BTS Composici13n de Historias Gr. 1-3
SSN1-256	Bud, Not Buddy NS Gr. 4-6
SSB1-31	Bugs, Bugs & More Bugs Gr. 2-3
SSR1-07	Building Word Families L.V. Gr. 1-2
SSR1-05	Building Word Families S.V. Gr. 1-2
SSN1-204	Bunnicula NS Gr. 4-6
SSB1-80	Butterflies & Caterpillars Gr. 1-2
SSN1-164	Call It Courage NS Gr. 7-8
SSN1-67	Call of the Wild NS Gr. 7-8
SSJ1-41	Canada & It's Trading Partners 6-8
SSPC-28	Canada B/W Pictures
SSN1-173	Canada Geese Quilt NS Gr. 4-6
SSJ1-01	Canada Gr. 1
SSJ1-33	Canada's Capital Cities Gr. 4-6
SSJ1-43	Canada's Confederation Gr. 7-8
SSF1-04	Canada's First Nations Gr. 7-8
SSJ1-51	Canada's Landmarks Gr. 1-3
SSJ1-48	Canada's Landmarks Gr. 4-6
SSJ1-60	Canada's Links to the World Gr. 5-8
SSJ1-42	Canada's Traditions & Celeb. Gr. 1-3
SSB1-45	Canadian Animals Gr. 1-2
SSJ1-37	Canadian Arctic Inuit Gr. 2-3
SSJ1-53	Canadian Black History Gr. 4-8
SSJ1-57	Canadian Comprehension Gr. 1-2
SSJ1-58	Canadian Comprehension Gr. 3-4
SSJ1-59	Canadian Comprehension Gr. 5-6
SSJ1-46	Canadian Industries Gr. 4-6
SSK1-12	Canadian Problem Solving Gr. 4-6
SSJ1-38	Canadian Provinces & Terr. Gr. 4-6
SSY1-07	Capitalization & Punctuation Gr. 1-3
SSN1-198	Captain Courageous NS Gr. 7-8
SSK1-11	Cars Problem Solving Gr. 3-4
SSN1-154	Castle in the Attic NS Gr. 4-6
SSF1-31	Castles & Kings Gr. 4-6
SSN1-144	Cat Ate My Gymsuit NS Gr. 4-6
SSPC-38	Cats B/W Pictures
SSB1-50	Cats – Domestic & Wild Gr. 4-6
SSN1-34	Cats in Literature Gr. 3-6
SSN1-212	Cay NS Gr. 7-8
SSM1-09	Celebrate Autumn Gr. 4-6
SSC1-39	Celebrate Christmas Gr. 4-6
SSC1-31	Celebrate Easter Gr. 4-6
SSC1-23	Celebrate Shamrock Day Gr. 2
SSM1-11	Celebrate Spring Gr. 4-6
SSC1-13	Celebrate Thanksgiving R. 3-4
SSM1-06	Celebrate Winter Gr. 4-6
SSB1-107	Cells, Tissues & Organs Gr. 7-8
SSB1-101	Characteristics of Flight Gr. 4-6
SSN1-66	Charlie & Chocolate Factory NS Gr. 4-6
SSN1-23	Charlotte's Web NS Gr. 4-6
SSB1-37	Chicks N'Ducks Gr. 2-4
SSA1-09	China Today Gr. 5-8
SSN1-70	Chocolate Fever NS Gr. 4-6
SSN1-241	Chocolate Touch NS Gr. 4-6
SSC1-38	Christmas Around the World Gr. 4-6
SSPC-42	Christmas B/W Pictures
SST1-08A	Christmas Gr. JK/SK
SST1-08B	Christmas Gr. 1
SST1-08C	Christmas Gr. 2-3
SSC1-04	Christmas Magic Gr. 1
SSC1-03	Christmas Tales Gr. 2-3
SSG1-06	Cinematography Gr. 5-8
SSPC-13	Circus B/W Pictures
SSF1-03	Circus Magic Gr. 3-4
SSJ1-52	Citizenship/Immigration Gr. 4-8
SSN1-104	Classical Poetry Gr. 7-12
SSN1-227	Color Gr. 1-3
SSN1-203	Colour Gr. 1-3
SSN1-135	Come Back Amelia Bedelia NS 1-3
SSH1-11	Community Helpers Gr. 1-3
SSK1-02	Concept Cards & Activities Gr. P-1
SSN1-183	Copper Sunrise NS Gr. 7-8
SSN1-86	Corduroy & Pocket Corduroy NS 1-3
SSN1-124	Could Dracula Live in Wood NS 4-6
SSN1-148	Cowboy's Don't Cry NS Gr. 7-8
SSR1-01	Creativity with Food Gr. 4-8
SSB1-34	Creatures of the Sea Gr. 2-4
SSN1-208	Curse of the Viking Grave NS 7-8
SSN1-134	Danny Champion of World NS 4-6
SSN1-98	Danny's Run NS Gr. 7-8
SSK1-21	Data Management Gr. 4-6
SSB1-53	Dealing with Dinosaurs Gr. 4-6
SSN1-178	Dear Mr. Henshaw NS Gr. 4-6
SSB1-22	Deer Gr. 3-5
SSPC-20	Desert B/W Pictures
SSJ1-40	Development of Western Canada 7-8
SSA1-16	Development of Manufacturing 7-9
SSN1-105	Dicken's Christmas NS Gr. 7-8
SSN1-62	Different Dragons NS Gr. 4-6
SSPC-21	Dinosaurs B/W Pictures
SSB1-16	Dinosaurs Gr. 1
SST1-02A	Dinosaurs Gr. JK/SK
SST1-02B	Dinosaurs Gr. 1
SST1-02 C	Dinosaurs Gr. 2-3
SSN1-175	Dinosaurs in Literature Gr. 1-3
SSJ1-26	Discover Nova Scotia Gr. 5-7
SSJ1-36	Discover Nunavut Territory Gr. 5-7
SSJ1-25	Discover Ontario Gr. 5-7
SSJ1-24	Discover PEI Gr. 5-7
SSJ1-22	Discover Québec Gr. 5-7
SSL1-01	Discovering the Library Gr. 2-3
SSB1-106	Diversity of Living Things Gr. 4-6
SSK1-27	Division Drills Gr. 4-6
SSB1-30	Dogs – Wild & Tame Gr. 4-6
SSPC-31	Dogs B/W Pictures
SSN1-196	Dog's Don't Tell Jokes NS Gr. 4-6
SSN1-182	Door in the Wall NS Gr. 4-6
SSB1-87	Down by the Sea Gr. 1-3
SSN1-189	Dr. Jeckyll & Mr. Hyde NS Gr. 4-6
SSG1-07	Dragon Trivia Gr. P-8
SSN1-102	Dragon's Egg NS Gr. 4-6
SSN1-16	Dragons in Literature Gr. 3-6
SSC1-06	Early Christmas Gr. 3-5
SSB1-109	Earth's Crust Gr. 6-8
SSC1-21	Easter Adventures Gr. 3-4
SSC1-17	Easter Delights Gr. P-K
SSC1-19	Easter Surprises Gr. 1
SSPC-12	Egypt B/W Pictures
SSN1-255	Egypt Game NS Gr. 4-6
SSF1-28	Egyptians Today & Yesterday Gr. 2-3
SSJ1-49	Elections in Canada Gr. 4-8
SSB1-108	Electricity Gr. 4-6
SSN1-02	Elves & the Shoemaker NS Gr. 1-3
SSH1-14	Emotions Gr. P-2
SSB1-85	Energy Gr. 4-6
SSN1-108	English Language Gr. 10-12
SSN1-156	Enjoying Eric Wilson Series Gr. 5-7
SSB1-64	Environment Gr. 4-6
SSR1-12	ESL Teaching Ideas Gr. K-8
SSN1-258	Esperanza Rising NS Gr. 4-6
SSR1-22	Exercises in Grammar Gr. 6
SSR1-23	Exercises in Grammar Gr. 7
SSR1-24	Exercises in Grammar Gr. 8
SSF1-20	Exploration Gr. 4-6
SSF1-15	Explorers & Mapmakers of Can. 7-8
SSJ1-54	Exploring Canada Gr. 1-3
SSJ1-56	Exploring Canada Gr. 1-6
SSJ1-55	Exploring Canada Gr. 4-6
SSH1-20	Exploring My School & Community 1
SSPC-39	Fables B/W Pictures
SSN1-15	Fables Gr. 4-6
SSN1-04	Fairy Tale Magic Gr. 3-5
SSPC-11	Fairy Tales B/W Pictures
SSN1-11	Fairy Tales Gr. 1-2
SSN1-199	Family Under the Bridge NS Gr. 4-6
SSPC-41	Famous Canadians B/W Pictures
SSJ1-12	Famous Canadians Gr. 4-8
SSN1-210	Fantastic Mr. Fox NS Gr. 4-6
SSB1-36	Fantastic Plants Gr. 4-6
SSPC-04	Farm Animals B/W Pictures
SSB1-15	Farm Animals Gr. 1-2
SST1-03A	Farm Gr. JK/SK
SST1-03B	Farm Gr. 1
SST1-03C	Farm Gr. 2-3
SSJ1-05	Farming Community Gr. 3-4
SSB1-44	Farmyard Friends Gr. P-K
SSJ1-45	Fathers of Confederation Gr. 4-8
SSB1-19	Feathered Friends Gr. 4-6
SST1-05A	February Gr. JK/SK
SST1-05B	February Gr. 1
SST1-05C	February Gr. 2-3
SSN1-03	Festival of Fairytales Gr. 3-5
SSC1-36	Festivals Around the World Gr. 2-3
SSN1-168	First 100 Sight Words Gr. 1
SSC1-32	First Days at School Gr. 1
SSJ1-06	Fishing Community Gr. 3-4
SSN1-170	Flowers for Algernon NS Gr. 7-8
SSN1-261	Flat Stanley NS Gr. 1-3
SSN1-128	Fly Away Home NS Gr. 4-6
SSD1-05	Food: Fact, Fun & Fiction Gr. 1-3
SSD1-06	Food: Nutrition & Invention Gr. 4-6
SSB1-118	Force and Motion Gr. 1-3
SSB1-119	Force and Motion Gr. 4-6
SSB1-25	Foxes Gr. 3-5
SSN1-263	Fractured Fairy Tales NS Gr. 1-3
SSN1-172	Freckle Juice NS Gr. 1-3
SSB1-43	Friendly Frogs Gr. 1
SSN1-260	Frindle NS Gr. 4-6
SSB1-89	Fruits & Seeds Gr. 4-6
SSN1-137	Fudge-a-Mania NS Gr. 4-6
SSB1-14	Fun on the Farm Gr. 3-4
SSR1-49	Fun with Phonics Gr. 1-3
SSPC-06	Garden Flowers B/W Pictures
SSK1-03	Geometric Shapes Gr. 2-5
SSC1-18	Get the Rabbit Habit Gr. 1-2
SSN1-209	Giver, The NS Gr. 7-8
SSN1-190	Go Jump in the Pool NS Gr. 4-6
SSG1-03	Goal Setting Gr. 6-8
SSG1-08	Gr. 3 Test – Parent Guide
SSG1-99	Gr. 3 Test – Teacher Guide
SSG1-09	Gr. 6 Language Test–Parent Guide
SSG1-97	Gr. 6 Language Test–Teacher Guide
SSG1-10	Gr. 6 Math Test – Parent Guide
SSG1-96	Gr. 6 Math Test – Teacher Guide
SSG1-98	Gr. 6 Math/Lang. Test–Teacher Guide
SSK1-14	Graph for all Seasons Gr. 1-3
SSN1-117	Great Brain NS Gr. 4-6
SSN1-90	Great Expectations NS Gr. 7-8
SSN1-169	Great Gilly Hopkins NS Gr. 4-6
SSN1-197	Great Science Fair Disaster NS Gr. 4-6
SSN1-138	Greek Mythology Gr. 7-8
SSN1-113	Green Gables Detectives NS 4-6
SSC1-26	Groundhog Celebration Gr. 2
SSC1-25	Groundhog Day Gr. 1
SSB1-113	Growth & Change in Animals Gr. 2-3
SSB1-114	Growth & Change in Plants Gr. 2-3
SSB1-48	Guinea Pigs & Friends Gr. 3-5
SSB1-104	Habitats Gr. 4-6
SSPC-18	Halloween B/W Pictures
SST1-04A	Halloween Gr. JK/SK
SST1-04B	Halloween Gr. 1
SST1-04C	Halloween Gr. 2-3
SSC1-10	Halloween Gr. 4-6
SSC1-08	Halloween Happiness Gr. 1
SSC1-29	Halloween Spirits Gr. P-K
SSY1-13	Handwriting Manuscript Gr 1-3
SSY1-14	Handwriting Cursive Gr. 1-3
SSC1-42	Happy Valentines Day Gr. 3
SSN1-205	Harper Moon NS Gr. 7-8
SSN1-123	Harriet the Spy NS Gr. 4-6
SSC1-11	Harvest Time Wonders Gr. 1
SSN1-136	Hatchet NS Gr. 7-8
SSC1-09	Haunting Halloween Gr. 2-3
SSN1-91	Hawk & Stretch NS Gr. 4-6
SSC1-30	Hearts & Flowers Gr. P-K
SSN1-22	Heidi NS Gr. 4-6
SSN1-120	Help I'm Trapped in My NS Gr. 4-6
SSN1-24	Henry & the Clubhouse NS Gr. 4-6
SSN1-184	Hobbit NS Gr. 7-8
SSN1-122	Hoboken Chicken Emerg. NS 4-6
SSN1-250	Holes NS Gr. 4-6
SSN1-116	How Can a Frozen Detective NS 4-6
SSN1-89	How Can I be a Detective if I NS 4-6
SSN1-96	How Come the Best Clues... NS 4-6

Publication Listing

Code #	Title and Grade
SSN1-133	How To Eat Fried Worms NS Gr.4-6
SSR1-48	How To Give a Presentation Gr. 4-6
SSN1-125	How To Teach Writing Through 7-9
SSR1-10	How To Write a Composition 6-10
SSR1-09	How To Write a Paragraph 5-10
SSR1-08	How To Write an Essay Gr. 7-12
SSR1-03	How To Write Poetry & Stories 4-6
SSD1-07	Human Body Gr. 2-4
SSD1-02	Human Body Gr. 4-6
SSN1-25	I Want to Go Home NS Gr. 4-6
SSH1-06	I'm Important Gr. 2-3
SSH1-07	I'm Unique Gr. 4-6
SSF1-05	In Days of Yore Gr. 4-6
SSF1-06	In Pioneer Days Gr. 2-4
SSM1-10	In the Wintertime Gr. 2
SSB1-41	Incredible Dinosaurs Gr. P-1
SSN1-177	Incredible Journey NS Gr. 4-6
SSN1-100	Indian in the Cupboard NS Gr. 4-6
SSPC-05	Insects B/W Pictures
SSPC-10	Inuit B/W Pictures
SSJ1-10	Inuit Community Gr. 3-4
SSN1-85	Ira Sleeps Over NS Gr. 1-3
SSN1-93	Iron Man NS Gr. 4-6
SSN1-193	Island of the Blue Dolphins NS 4-6
SSB1-11	It's a Dogs World Gr. 2-3
SSM1-05	It's a Marshmallow World Gr. 3
SSK1-05	It's About Time Gr. 2-4
SSC1-41	It's Christmas Time Gr. 3
SSH1-04	It's Circus Time Gr. 1
SSC1-43	It's Groundhog Day Gr. 3
SSB1-75	It's Maple Syrup Time Gr. 2-4
SSC1-40	It's Trick or Treat Time Gr. 2
SSN1-65	James & The Giant Peach NS 4-6
SSN1-106	Jane Eyre NS Gr. 7-8
SSPC-25	Japan B/W Pictures
SSA1-06	Japan Gr. 5-8
SSN1-264	Journey to the Centre of the Earth NS Gr. 7-8
SSC1-05	Joy of Christmas Gr. 2
SSN1-161	Julie of the Wolves NS Gr. 7-8
SSB1-81	Jungles Gr. 2-3
SSE1-02	Junior Music for Fall Gr. 4-6
SSE1-05	Junior Music for Spring Gr. 4-6
SSE1-06	Junior Music for Winter Gr. 4-6
SSR1-62	Just for Boys - Reading Comprehension Gr. 3-6
SSR1-63	Just for Boys - Reading Comprehension Gr. 6-8
SSN1-151	Kate NS Gr. 4-6
SSN1-95	Kidnapped in the Yukon NS Gr. 4-6
SSN1-140	Kids at Bailey School Gr. 2-4
SSN1-176	King of the Wind NS Gr. 4-6
SSF1-29	Klondike Gold Rush Gr. 4-6
SSF1-33	Labour Movement in Canada Gr. 7-8
SSN1-152	Lamplighter NS Gr. 4-6
SSB1-98	Learning About Dinosaurs Gr. 3
SSN1-38	Learning About Giants Gr. 4-6
SSK1-22	Learning About Measurement Gr. 1-3
SSB1-46	Learning About Mice Gr. 3-5
SSK1-09	Learning About Money CDN Gr. 1-3
SSK1-19	Learning About Money USA Gr. 1-3
SSK1-23	Learning About Numbers Gr. 1-3
SSB1-69	Learning About Rocks & Soils Gr. 2-3
SSK1-08	Learning About Shapes Gr. 1-3
SSB1-100	Learning About Simple Machines 1-3
SSK1-04	Learning About the Calendar Gr. 2-3
SSK1-10	Learning About Time Gr. 1-3
SSH1-17	Learning About Transportation Gr. 1
SSB1-02	Leaves Gr. 2-3
SSN1-50	Legends Gr. 4-6
SSC1-27	Lest We Forget Gr. 4-6
SSJ1-13	Let's Look at Canada Gr. 4-6
SSJ1-16	Let's Visit Alberta Gr. 2-4
SSJ1-15	Let's Visit British Columbia Gr. 2-4
SSJ1-03	Let's Visit Canada Gr. 3
SSJ1-18	Let's Visit Manitoba Gr. 2-4
SSJ1-21	Let's Visit New Brunswick Gr. 2-4
SSJ1-27	Let's Visit NFLD & Labrador Gr. 2-4
SSJ1-30	Let's Visit North West Terr. Gr. 2-4
SSJ1-20	Let's Visit Nova Scotia Gr. 2-4
SSJ1-34	Let's Visit Nunavut Gr. 2-4
SSJ1-17	Let's Visit Ontario Gr. 2-4
SSQ1-08	Let's Visit Ottawa Big Book Pkg 1-3
SSJ1-19	Let's Visit PEI Gr. 2-4
SSJ1-31	Let's Visit Québec Gr. 2-4
SSJ1-14	Let's Visit Saskatchewan Gr. 2-4
SSJ1-28	Let's Visit Yukon Gr. 2-4
SSN1-130	Life & Adv. of Santa Claus NS 7-8
SSB1-10	Life in a Pond Gr. 3-4
SSF1-30	Life in the Middle Ages Gr. 7-8
SSB1-103	Light & Sound Gr. 4-6
SSN1-219	Light in the Forest NS Gr. 7-8
SSN1-121	Light on Hogback Hill NS Gr. 4-6
SSN1-46	Lion, Witch & the Wardrobe NS 4-6
SSR1-51	Literature Response Forms Gr. 1-3
SSR1-52	Literature Response Forms Gr. 4-6
SSN1-28	Little House Big Woods NS 4-6
SSN1-233	Little House on the Prairie NS 4-6
SSN1-111	Little Women NS Gr. 7-8
SSN1-115	Live from the Fifth Grade NS 4-6
SSN1-141	Look Through My Window NS 4-6
SSN1-112	Look! Visual Discrimination Gr. P-1
SSN1-61	Lost & Found NS Gr. 4-6
SSN1-109	Lost in the Barrens NS Gr. 7-8
SSJ1-08	Lumbering Community Gr. 3-4
SSN1-167	Magic School Bus Gr. 1-3
SSN1-247	Magic Treehouse Gr. 1-3
SSB1-78	Magnets Gr. 3-5
SSD1-03	Making Sense of Our Senses K-1
SSN1-146	Mama's Going to Buy You a NS 4-6
SSB1-94	Mammals Gr. 1
SSB1-95	Mammals Gr. 2
SSB1-96	Mammals Gr. 3
SSB1-97	Mammals Gr. 5-6
SSN1-160	Maniac Magee NS Gr. 4-6
SSA1-19	Mapping Activities & Outlines! 4-8
SSA1-17	Mapping Skills Gr. 1-3
SSA1-07	Mapping Skills Gr. 4-6
SST1-10A	March Gr. JK/SK
SST1-10B	March Gr. 1
SST1-10C	March Gr. 2-3
SSB1-57	Marvellous Marsupials Gr. 4-6
SSK1-01	Math Signs & Symbols Gr. 1-3
SSB1-116	Matter & Materials Gr. 1-3
SSB1-117	Matter & Materials Gr. 4-6
SSH1-03	Me, I'm Special! Gr. P-1
SSK1-16	Measurement Gr. 4-8
SSC1-02	Medieval Christmas Gr. 4-6
SSPC-09	Medieval Life B/W Pictures
SSC1-07	Merry Christmas Gr. P-K
SSK1-15	Metric Measurement Gr. 4-8
SSN1-13	Mice in Literature Gr. 3-5
SSB1-70	Microscopy Gr. 4-6
SSN1-180	Midnight Fox NS Gr. 4-6
SSN1-243	Midwife's Apprentice NS Gr. 4-6
SSJ1-07	Mining Community Gr. 3-4
SSK1-17	Money Talks – Cdn Gr. 3-6
SSK1-18	Money Talks – USA Gr. 3-6
SSB1-56	Monkeys & Apes Gr. 4-6
SSN1-43	Monkeys in Literature Gr. 2-4
SSN1-54	Monster Mania Gr. 4-6
SSN1-97	Mouse & the Motorcycle NS 4-6
SSN1-94	Mr. Poppers Penguins NS Gr. 4-6
SSN1-201	Mrs. Frisby & Rats NS Gr. 4-6
SSR1-13	Milti-Level Spelling Program Gr. 3-6
SSR1-26	Multi-Level Spelling USA Gr. 3-6
SSK1-31	Addition & Subtraction Drills 1-3
SSK1-32	Multiplication & Division Drills 4-6
SSK1-30	Multiplication Drills Gr. 4-6
SSA1-14	My Country! The USA! Gr. 2-4
SSN1-186	My Side of the Mountain NS 7-8
SSN1-58	Mysteries, Monsters & Magic Gr. 6-8
SSN1-37	Mystery at Blackrock Island NS 7-8
SSN1-80	Mystery House NS 4-6
SSN1-157	Nate the Great & Sticky Case NS 1-3
SSF1-23	Native People of North America 4-6
SSF1-25	New France Part 1 Gr. 7-8
SSF1-27	New France Part 2 Gr. 7-8
SSA1-10	New Zealand Gr. 4-8
SSN1-51	Newspapers Gr. 5-8
SSN1-47	No Word for Goodbye NS Gr. 7-8
SSPC-03	North American Animals B/W Pictures
SSF1-22	North American Natives Gr. 2-4
SSN1-75	Novel Ideas Gr. 4-6
SST1-06A	November JK/SK
SST1-06B	November Gr. 1
SST1-06C	November Gr. 2-3
SSN1-244	Number the Stars NS Gr. 4-6
SSY1-03	Numeration Gr. 1-3
SSPC-14	Nursery Rhymes B/W Pictures
SSN1-12	Nursery Rhymes Gr. P-1
SSN1-59	On the Banks of Plum Creek NS 4-6
SSN1-220	One in Middle Green Kangaroo NS 1-3
SSN1-145	One to Grow On NS Gr. 4-6
SSB1-27	Opossums Gr. 3-5
SSJ1-23	Ottawa Gr. 7-9
SSJ1-39	Our Canadian Governments Gr. 5-8
SSF1-14	Our Global Heritage Gr. 4-6
SSH1-12	Our Neighbourhoods Gr. 4-6
SSB1-72	Our Trash Gr. 2-3
SSB1-51	Our Universe Gr. 5-8
SSB1-86	Outer Space Gr. 1-2
SSA1-18	Outline Maps of the World Gr. 1-8
SSB1-67	Owls Gr. 4-6
SSN1-31	Owls in the Family NS Gr. 4-6
SSL1-02	Oxbridge Owl & The Library Gr. 4-6
SSB1-71	Pandas, Polar & Penguins Gr. 4-6
SSN1-52	Paperbag Princess NS Gr. 1-3
SSR1-11	Passion of Jesus: A Play Gr. 7-8
SSA1-12	Passport to Adventure Gr. 4-5
SSR1-06	Passport to Adventure Gr. 7-8
SSR1-04	Personal Spelling Dictionary Gr. 2-5
SSPC-29	Pets B/W Pictures
SSE1-03	Phantom of the Opera Gr. 7-9
SSN1-171	Phoebe Gilman Author Study Gr. 2-3
SSY1-06	Phonics Gr. 1-3
SSK1-33	Picture Math Book Gr. 1-3
SSN1-237	Pierre Berton Author Study Gr. 7-8
SSN1-179	Pigman NS Gr. 7-8
SSN1-48	Pigs in Literature Gr. 2-4
SSN1-99	Pinballs NS Gr. 4-6
SSN1-60	Pippi Longstocking NS Gr. 4-6
SSF1-12	Pirates Gr. 4-6
SSK1-13	Place Value Gr. 4-6
SSB1-77	Planets Gr. 3-6
SSR1-74	Poetry Prompts Gr. 1-3
SSR1-75	Poetry Prompts Gr. 4-6
SSB1-66	Popcorn Fun Gr. 2-3
SSB1-20	Porcupines Gr. 3-5
SSR1-55	Practice Manuscript Gr. Pk-2
SSR1-56	Practice Cursive Gr. 2-4
SSF1-24	Prehistoric Times Gr. 4-6
SSE1-01	Primary Music for Fall Gr. 1-3
SSE1-04	Primary Music for Spring Gr. 1-3
SSE1-07	Primary Music for Winter Gr. 1-3
SSJ1-47	Prime Ministers of Canada Gr. 4-8
SSN1-262	Prince Caspian NS Gr. 4-6
SSK1-20	Probability & Inheritance Gr. 7-10
SSN1-49	Question of Loyalty NS Gr. 7-8
SSN1-26	Rabbits in Literature Gr. 2-4
SSB1-17	Raccoons Gr. 3-5
SSN1-207	Radio Fifth Grade NS Gr. 4-6
SSB1-52	Rainbow of Colours Gr. 4-6
SSN1-144	Ramona Quimby Age 8 NS 4-6
SSJ1-09	Ranching Community Gr. 3-4
SSY1-08	Reading for Meaning Gr. 1-3
SSR1-76	Reading Logs Gr. K-1
SSR1-77	Reading Logs Gr. 2-3
SSN1-165	Reading Response Forms Gr. 1-3
SSN1-239	Reading Response Forms Gr. 4-6
SSN1-234	Reading with Arthur Gr. 1-3
SSN1-249	Reading with Canadian Authors 1-3
SSN1-200	Reading with Curious George Gr. 2-4
SSN1-230	Reading with Eric Carle Gr. 1-3
SSN1-251	Reading with Kenneth Oppel Gr. 4-6
SSN1-127	Reading with Mercer Mayer Gr. 1-2
SSN1-07	Reading with Motley Crew Gr. 2-3
SSN1-142	Reading with Robert Munsch 1-3
SSN1-06	Reading with the Super Sleuths 4-6
SSN1-08	Reading with the Ziggles Gr. 1
SST1-11A	Red Gr. JK/SK
SSN1-147	Refuge NS Gr. 7-8
SSC1-44	Remembrance Day Gr. 1-3
SSPC-23	Reptiles B/W Pictures
SSB1-42	Reptiles Gr. 4-6
SSN1-110	Return of the Indian NS Gr. 4-6
SSN1-225	River NS Gr. 7-8
SSE1-08	Robert Schuman, Composer Gr. 6-9
SSN1-83	Robot Alert NS Gr. 4-6
SSB1-65	Rocks & Minerals Gr. 4-6
SSN1-149	Romeo & Juliet NS Gr. 7-8
SSB1-88	Romping Reindeer Gr. K-3
SSN1-21	Rumplestiltskin NS Gr. 1-3
SSN1-153	Runaway Ralph NS Gr. 4-6
SSN1-103	Sadako & 1000 Paper Cranes NS 4-6
SSD1-04	Safety Gr. 2-4
SSN1-42	Sarah Plain & Tall NS Gr. 4-6
SSC1-34	School in September Gr. 4-6
SSPC-01	Sea Creatures B/W Pictures
SSB1-79	Sea Creatures Gr. 1-3
SSN1-64	Secret Garden NS Gr. 4-6
SSB1-90	Seeds & Weeds Gr. 2-3
SSY1-02	Sentence Writing Gr. 1-3
SST1-07A	September JK/SK
SST1-07B	September Gr. 1
SST1-07C	September Gr. 2-3
SSN1-30	Serendipity Series Gr. 3-5
SSC1-22	Shamrocks on Parade Gr. 1
SSC1-24	Shamrocks, Harps & Shillelaghs 3-4
SSR1-66	Shakespeare Shorts-Perf Arts Gr. 1-4
SSR1-67	Shakespeare Shorts-Perf Arts Gr. 4-6
SSR1-68	Shakespeare Shorts-Lang Arts Gr. 2-4
SSR1-69	Shakespeare Shorts-Lang Arts Gr. 4-6
SSB1-74	Sharks Gr. 4-6
SSN1-158	Shiloh NS Gr. 4-6
SSN1-84	Sideways Stories Wayside NS 4-6
SSN1-181	Sight Words Activities Gr. 1
SSB1-99	Simple Machines Gr. 4-6
SSN1-19	Sixth Grade Secrets 4-6
SSG1-04	Skill Building with Slates Gr. K-8
SSN1-118	Skinny Bones NS Gr. 4-6
SSB1-24	Skunks Gr. 3-5
SSN1-191	Sky is Falling NS Gr. 4-6
SSB1-83	Slugs & Snails Gr. 1-3
SSB1-55	Snakes Gr. 4-6
SST1-12A	Snow Gr. JK/SK
SST1-12B	Snow Gr. 1
SST1-12C	Snow Gr. 2-3
SSB1-76	Solar System Gr. 4-6
SSPC-44	South America B/W Pictures
SSA1-11	South America Gr. 4-6
SSB1-05	Space Gr. 2-3
SSR1-34	Spelling Blacklines Gr. 1
SSR1-35	Spelling Blacklines Gr. 2
SSR1-36	Spelling Blacklines Gr. 3
SSR1-37	Spelling Blacklines Gr. 4
SSR1-14	Spelling Gr. 1
SSR1-15	Spelling Gr. 2
SSR1-16	Spelling Gr. 3
SSR1-17	Spelling Gr. 4
SSR1-18	Spelling Gr. 5
SSR1-19	Spelling Gr. 6
SSR1-27	Spelling Worksavers #1 Gr. 3-5
SSM1-02	Spring Celebration Gr. 2-3
SST1-01A	Spring Gr. JK/SK
SST1-01B	Spring Gr. 1
SST1-01C	Spring Gr. 2-3
SSM1-01	Spring in the Garden Gr. 1-2
SSB1-26	Squirrels Gr. 3-5
SSB1-112	Stable Structures & Mechanisms 3
SSG1-05	Steps in the Research Process 5-8
SSG1-02	Stock Market Gr. 7-8
SSN1-139	Stone Fox NS Gr. 4-6
SSN1-214	Stone Orchard NS Gr. 7-8
SSN1-01	Story Book Land of Witches Gr. 2-3
SSR1-64	Story Starters Gr. 1-3
SSR1-65	Story Starters Gr. 4-6
SSR1-73	Story Starters Gr. 1-6
SSY1-09	Story Writing Gr. 1-3
SSB1-111	Structures, Mechanisms & Motion 2
SSN1-211	Stuart Little NS Gr. 4-6
SSK1-29	Subtraction Drills Gr. 1-3
SSY1-05	Subtraction Gr. 1-3
SSY1-11	Successful Language Pract. Gr. 1-3
SSY1-12	Successful Math Practice Gr. 1-3
SSW1-09	Summer Learning Gr. K-1
SSW1-10	Summer Learning Gr. 1-2
SSW1-11	Summer Learning Gr. 2-3
SSW1-12	Summer Learning Gr. 3-4
SSW1-13	Summer Learning Gr. 4-5
SSW1-14	Summer Learning Gr. 5-6
SSN1-159	Summer of the Swans NS Gr. 4-6
SSZ1-02	Summer Olympics Gr. 4-6
SSM1-07	Super Summer Gr. 1-2
SSN1-18	Superfudge NS Gr. 4-6
SSA1-08	Switzerland Gr. 4-6
SSN1-20	T.V. Kid NS. Gr. 4-6
SSA1-15	Take a Trip to Australia Gr. 2-3
SSB1-102	Taking Off With Flight Gr. 1-3
SSK1-34	Teaching Math with Everyday Munipulatives Gr. 4-6
SSN1-259	The Tale of Despereaux NS Gr. 4-6
SSN1-55	Tales of the Fourth Grade NS 4-6
SSN1-188	Taste of Blackberries NS Gr. 4-6
SSK1-07	Teaching Math Through Sports 6-9
SST1-09A	Thanksgiving JK/SK
SST1-09C	Thanksgiving Gr. 2-3
SSN1-77	There's a Boy in the Girls... NS 4-6
SSN1-143	This Can't Be Happening NS 4-6
SSN1-05	Three Billy Goats Gruff NS Gr. 1-3
SSN1-72	Ticket to Curlew NS Gr. 4-6
SSN1-82	Timothy of the Cay NS Gr. 7-8
SSF1-32	Titanic Gr. 4-6
SSN1-222	To Kill a Mockingbird NS Gr. 7-8
SSN1-195	Toilet Paper Tigers NS Gr. 4-6
SSJ1-35	Toronto Gr. 4-8
SSH1-02	Toy Shelf Gr. P-K
SSPC-24	Toys B/W Pictures
SSN1-163	Traditional Poetry Gr. 7-10
SSH1-13	Transportation Gr. 4-6
SSW1-01	Transportation Snip Art
SSB1-03	Trees Gr. 2-3
SSA1-01	Tropical Rainforest Gr. 4-6
SSN1-56	Trumpet of the Swan NS Gr. 4-6
SSN1-81	Tuck Everlasting NS Gr. 4-6
SSN1-126	Turtles in Literature Gr. 1-3
SSN1-45	Underground to Canada NS 4-6

Publication Listing

Code #	Title and Grade
SSN1-27	Unicorns in Literature Gr. 3-5
SSJ1-44	Upper & Lower Canada Gr. 7-8
SSN1-192	Using Novels Canadian North Gr. 7-8
SSC1-14	Valentines Day Gr. 5-8
SSPC-45	Vegetables B/W Pictures
SSY1-01	Very Hungry Caterpillar NS 30/Pkg Gr. 1-3
SSF1-13	Victorian Era Gr. 7-8
SSC1-35	Victorian Christmas Gr. 5-8
SSF1-17	Viking Age Gr. 4-6
SSN1-206	War with Grandpa SN Gr. 4-6
SSB1-91	Water Gr. 2-4
SSN1-166	Watership Down NS Gr. 7-8
SSH1-16	Ways We Travel Gr. P-K
SSN1-101	Wayside Sch. Little Stranger NS Gr. 4-6
SSN1-76	Wayside Sch. is Falling Down NS 4-6
SSB1-60	Weather Gr. 4-6
SSN1-17	Wee Folk in Literature Gr. 3-5
SSPC-08	Weeds B/W Pictures
SSQ1-04	Welcome Back – Big Book Pkg 1-3
SSB1-73	Whale Preservation Gr. 5-8
SSH1-08	What is a Community? Gr. 2-4
SSH1-01	What is a Family? Gr. 2-3
SSH1-09	What is a School? Gr. 1-2
SSJ1-32	What is Canada? Gr. P-K
SSN1-79	What is RAD? Read & Discover 2-4
SSB1-62	What is the Weather Today? Gr. 2-4
SSN1-194	What's a Daring Detective NS 4-6
SSH1-10	What's My Number Gr. P-K
SSR1-02	What's the Scoop on Words Gr. 4-6
SSN1-73	Where the Red Fern Grows NS Gr. 7-8
SSN1-87	Where the Wild Things Are NS Gr. 1-3
SSN1-187	Whipping Boy NS Gr. 4-6
SSN1-226	Who is Frances Rain? NS Gr. 4-6
SSN1-74	Who's Got Gertie & How...? NS Gr. 4-6
SSN1-131	Why did the Underwear ... NS 4-6
SSC1-28	Why Wear a Poppy? Gr. 2-3
SSJ1-11	Wild Animals of Canada Gr. 2-3
SSPC-07	Wild Flowers B/W Pictures
SSB1-18	Winter Birds Gr. 2-3
SSZ1-03	Winter Olympics Gr. 4-6
SSM1-04	Winter Wonderland Gr. 1
SSC1-01	Witches Gr. 3-4
SSN1-213	Wolf Island NS Gr. 1-3
SSE1-09	Wolfgang Amadeus Mozart 6-9
SSB1-23	Wolves Gr. 3-5
SSC1-20	Wonders of Easter Gr. 2
SSY1-15	Word Families Gr. 1-3
SSR1-59	Word Families 2,3 Letter Words Gr. 1-3
SSR1-60	Word Families 3, 4 Letter Words Gr. 1-3
SSR1-61	Word Families 2, 3, 4 Letter Words Big Book Gr. 1-3
SSB1-35	World of Horses Gr. 4-6
SSB1-13	World of Pets Gr. 2-3
SSF1-26	World War II Gr. 7-8
SSN1-221	Wrinkle in Time NS Gr. 7-8
SSPC-02	Zoo Animals B/W Pictures
SSB1-08	Zoo Animals Gr. 1-2
SSB1-09	Zoo Celebration Gr. 3-4